HONOUR BOUND

HONOUR BOUND

THEODORE BELCASTRO

FIRST EDITION

Copyright @ Theodore Belcastro, 2025

No part of this book may be reproduced in any manner whatsoever without written permission except in the case of brief quotations embodied in critical articles and reviews.

All Rights Reserved

This is a work of fiction.
Names, characters, places and incidents originate from the writer's imagination. Any resemblance to actual persons, living or dead, is purely coincidental.

https://theobelcastro.wixsite.com/theodore-belcastro

First Published in **2025**

Anchora Press

Other Novels by the Author

The Call of Magic
Raven's Masquerade

Coming Soon...

Blood & Wine
Fiction & Fables (Short Story Collection)

To my fellow authors,
May we navigate the publishing industry's absurdities with a well-earned sense of humour and a relentless belief that our stories will find their way to the people who need them.

A Note on Sequels

The publishing industry, bless its heart, loves a good sequel. A trilogy, a tetralogy, a sprawling series of twenty-seven-and-a-half tomes that can be repackaged and sold in boxed sets for all eternity. It's a dependable, unyielding thing, a genre as predictable as a winter cold. But dependable, as we know, is often just another word for dull.

This, then, is not a sequel.

One might notice the return of a world, perhaps even some familiar faces and places, from my first novel *The Call of Magic*. But one must understand that this world, Cymeria, like a particularly complicated bit of knitting, has simply been allowed to unravel and then sort of re-knit itself. Things have, as they so often do, gone on. The old heroes, if indeed one could call them that, have gone about their business. The villains have, with equal fervour, also gone about theirs. And the mundane, relentless rhythm of day-to-day existence has swallowed them all up like so much lumpy gruel.

No, this particular tale of swords and sorcery is merely another footnote in the great and terrible saga of things-that-happen-to-be-occurring in Cymeria. It's a story about the sort of man who finds himself standing in the wrong place at the wrong time, and with a rather grim sense of fatalistic obligation, decides to stay there for a bit. It's a story of honour, of duty, and of the profoundly inconvenient nature of both.

So, if you've come looking for a sequel, I'm afraid you'll be sorely disappointed. If, however, you've an appetite for a man with a gold tooth and a profound sense of world-weariness stumbling his way through an increasingly chaotic world, then please, read on. The rest, as they say, is just history repeating itself, as it always seems to do.

I

The Unkindness of Strangers

B ihan the Beauty wasted no time. His khopesh sang, an eerie, predatory hum of steel, as it cleaved his opponent's arm in one smooth stroke. In his off-hand, a jagged dagger—once a resplendent sword, now a vicious fragment—drove into the garnok's flank with merciless finality. A gentleman of some far-off, perfumed court might've called the move barbaric. Bihan knew the word well. He bore it like a name.

The aged black key at his neck pressed cool against his skin, its surface catching the midday sun as rivulets of salt sheen tracked down his forearms.

The garnok spat in his face, then snapped its scaly droptail with bone-jarring force. The thud sank into Bihan's bulging bicep, hurling him into the lichen-scarred frieze of the ruined acropolis. Ancient carvings, brittle with centuries, shattered beneath him. Phlegm smeared his jaw. The impact tore a gasp from his lungs, every muscle howling in protest. His molars cracked under the strain, another shattered tooth splintering across his tongue.

The coin was never enough. Not for greed. Never that. But for boredom. A crushing, marrow-deep boredom that gnawed and gnawed. Another day. Another kill.

He rose from dust and ruin, khopesh dragging shallow furrows as it hung from loose fingers. He winked at the garnok, slow and deliberate, mocking. These beasts—resilient and battle-hardened—had swarmed tenfold since magic had re-surfaced, raw power bleeding into the world and fuelling mercenary work across the known lands. Yet none had been as old, as brutal, as cunning as this one. Drop-tail garnoks were spoken of as lesser to their revered dragon-tailed kin.

Tavern talk. Fool's myths.

This garnok had butchered Fregor the Cutpurse, Bihan's companion, and carved a grotesque trail of corpses from the southern continent to his doorstep, defiling everything he loved, despite his homeland's rapid advancements. Across steppes and deserts, it'd extorted, plundered, slaughtered without restraint. And for enough dinero, Bihan would end its legacy, as always, with brutal precision.

"You fight well, Bihan Alihanson," the creature sneered, feline features twisting. Yellowed fangs gleamed, fresh blood clinging. "But you're not your father."

Bihan's jaw flexed. Old scars pulled taut. Dampness slid from his brow to his tartan kilt. Heat gathered beneath his ribs, boredom kindling into something sharper. He sank into a low, coiled stance: Alihan's stance drilled into his bones long ago. He beckoned with a crook of his thrice-broken finger.

The garnok roared, raising its double-edged axe. Sunlight licked the blade, wicked and clean. "Suffer me no longer, barbarian! Finish it or join Fregor in the dirt!"

Its snarl shredded the air, layered with pain and stubborn defiance.

Bihan feinted, lightning-quick, a deceptive flick towards its abdomen. A half-pivot, a blur. He lunged. The axe caught low, wrenching the khopesh down into sand with a clang. Buried to the hilt. Useless. The garnok pressed forwards, unshaken. What was one arm less to a beast born of war?

Bihan slipped behind a pillar, flowing like water. He sprang from its sloped edge, an arc of motion that shattered the garnok's nose beneath his sandal. Bone crunched. His knee followed, bursting its eye in a wet squelch. The broken blade spun once in his palm, then speared downwards into the sinewed neck. Blood bubbled. The creature choked, then chuckled. A sound drenched in defiance. It greeted Death with a smile; gaze fixed on endless sky. Whatever name it bore vanished unspoken. A great beast. Another slain. Nothing new.

Yet unease coiled in Bihan's gut. The garnok had known him. It'd welcomed the end. A stone-heavy doubt settled inside him—alien, unfamiliar, undeniable. Above, the southern sky was torn open: auroras slithered through bright daylight, an omen that belonged nowhere. The ashen-haired witch had fled into the mountains; prophecy's silhouette against the horizon. Childhood lessons of ruin, plague, and madness rose like smoke in his mind. Stories from his sept.

Bihan the Beauty felt misaligned. Not broken. Just... off. The garnok's smile lingered, a fragment of defiance, a signal of something larger. Soon the blue dusk of a changed world would bleed over the steppes like mourning silk. He needed a drink. A stinging draught to scour the taste of dust and death from his tongue.

Khopesh in hand, muscles taut, Bihan stepped forwards and severed the garnok's head from its shoulders. Proof was always demanded by contractors. Something final. Undeniable.

Returning to civilisation, his blood-soaked hessian sack stained the tartan of his clan, and Fregor's corpse hung across his shoulder like an icy burden. Bihan decided his first stop would be the surgeon to mend his broken tooth. Perhaps replace it with gold. He'd always fancied a golden one: brazen, showy. Then he'd claim payment for a job well done. Only then could he afford to bury Fregor properly.

Ironically, the night before, the cutpurse-turned-bard had sung of headstones carved in the Reaper's likeness—haunting shapes he found beautiful, like the dog-eared books he'd devoured: high adventures, rivers of blood, dark sorcery. As if he knew what waited. As if he'd breathed it in, a chill pre-science woven into the aether. Magic had re-surfaced, and perhaps it had awakened something dormant in them both. The world had shifted. Irrevocably. So too had its people.

Compelled to honour Fregor's last wishes, regardless of the ruinous cost, Bihan vowed it would be done. His companions were thieves, vagabonds, mercenaries, and they stank worse than a cesspit, yet they were his kin. A chosen family. A ragged brotherhood. The Circular City's graveyards were no marble labyrinths like those in grander places, but grim pockets of silence, touched with dignity. Fregor had always spoken of the one near the medial wall, where his parents lay. A sanctuary he'd claimed for himself.

Bihan lumbered through the narrow streets, craving space, a breath of solitude from the jostling crowds and oppressive closeness. He passed beneath sputtering neolyts whose erratic mana-light painted the grime in fits and starts. Defaced icons of the old ruling clan glared from walls, daubed with crude symbols, and above them a graffito screamed:

THE EMPRESS IS DEAD. LONG LIVE THE IMPERATOR.

From the southern gate northwards, the briny tang of ocean had faded, replaced by refuse, damp stone, and the salt of packed bodies. A suffocating pall. He despised the cloying stench of civilisation, the way it gnawed at his temper. Yet cities paid well. Some even commissioned him to sculpt a magnum opus of the Last Barbarian—irony not lost on him. In Aledhyn he could scarcely walk a block without a merchant begging for a rival's head, or some desperate man trying to barter his daughter for dinero. The city clung, demanding. It never let him simply be. Only the weight of Fregor's corpse bought him a measure of solitude, a grim buffer against the press of humanity.

Bihan had built a formidable reputation. He neither prized it nor scorned it; it simply was, shaping his life beyond undoing. Worse were the whispers of his private indulgences, pleasures he'd hoped to bury through bribes or promises. Once spoken, however, they defined him. But indulgence didn't buy burials. Or golden teeth. Only dinero did.

Had Fregor lived, he would've snorted, maybe tossed some cutting barb, when a desperate man pressed his daughter's henna-stained feet forwards as though they were coin enough. Small, tender things, dust clinging to the arches, the fading henna dye etching whorls across plump toes. Not gold. Not silver. A ridiculous gesture and one Fregor would've mocked without mercy. The thought coaxed a chuckle from Bihan, his split lips raw, the sound low and rasping in the stagnant air.

The surgeon's sandstone dwelling offered cool stillness after the clamour of the streets. He laid Fregor gently on a worn bench. From behind an embroidered curtain hobbled a squat garnok woman, tusks curved and ringed with silver, one eye emerald, the other clouded amber. Unease flickered through him... another of their kind. Yet no fury burnt in her gaze, only boredom. A trait Bihan could understand.

She worked swiftly, silent, asking nothing. Her touch was steady, her movements pared to ruthless efficiency. Fingers calloused from years of practice, their texture more like the soft, padded underside of a hound's paw than human flesh, anchored his jaw, and then one brutal wrench tore the molar free. A flash of pain shot through his skull, sharp enough to make his vision blur, iron flooding his tongue. Before the ache could settle, the gleam of gold was pressed into place. Crude rather than crafted, but it held, and its glint would draw wandering eyes away from the scars etched deep across his face.

Bihan turned, instinct tugging, as though Fregor might still offer a smirk or sly nod. Only blank eyes met him, glassy and unyielding. The ache behind his ribs flared sharp, a hollow wound no gold could fill. He missed Fregor. He missed Rabia the Rogue as well, though hers was a slower absence, dulled by distance and time. She still lived, entombed in coin, hemmed in by respectability, yet she might as well have been buried all the same. He'd not gone to her, bound tight to his brutal rhythm of labour and blood.

With a breath heavy as stone, he scattered his last coins across the surgeon's palm, shouldered Fregor's weight anew, and stepped into the streets. The air was a stew of sweat, brine, and smoke. Merchants barked, beggars whined, and the rasp of whetstones carried from shadowed alleys. The crush of bodies closed in, a tide of heat and noise that pressed against him, demanding, insistent, refusing him space to grieve.

A corpse slung over a mercenary's shoulder drew little notice in the underbelly. Here, life was a trinket, death its daily toll. Only in the inner city, where façades gleamed and order moved like a choreographed dance, would eyes widen or lips part in shock. Behind those polished doors crime dressed itself in velvet, perfumed with incense and false piety. Politicians, with their endless levies, were but thieves with ledgers, hands deep in every purse. Nobles were murderers cloaked in silk, their blades hidden beneath ceremony. And the ruling clan? Extortionists to the bone, draining the people's lifeblood drop by drop.

Bihan felt most at ease in the gutters, wrapped in the grit and the quiet anonymity of shadow. Here, a corpse was no spectacle but a passing detail, one dead man no different from the next. Life and death blurred into the same grey monotony, each exchange as common as dust in the wind. Business remained business, brutal and unchanging, though its constancy carried the sour taste of rot. And so, he pressed on, ready to claim his payment for a job well done, though the words rang hollow in a world that never stayed paid.

The contractor's house of trade oozed foulness.

A shiver crawled his spine, not from chill, but disgust. To call it an establishment was generous; it was a festering sore. Disease bred here, twinned with vice, and together they were passed like secrets from bed to bed. The pimp who ruled this ruin guarded such truths as jealously as coin, lest they corrode what remained of his thin, meticulously counted pockets.

A desperate, shivering mass clustered at the brothel's sides—beggars and thieves, their gaunt faces hollow-eyed, lit with hunger. They boiled sandals for nourishment, gnawing strips of gristled leather. Penniless, predatory, they prowled the perimeter, hoping to catch a sailor's bleary gaze or snatch a glinting gold coin "fallen" into their path.

"You look like *kheghch*!" the eunuch guardsman sneered, his voice reedy and thin for such a hulking frame. On indefinite loan from the inner-city harem, his unusual status came with baggage. He boasted often that his pillar and stones were intact. A claim Aledhyn's emirs didn't find amusing.

"And you smell like it," Bihan rasped, gravel in his tone. He ran his tongue over the new gold tooth, its smooth surface a strange comfort. "Where's Felipe?"

"No hello, no courtesy... Is that a gold tooth?" The eunuch squinted, curiosity overtaking duty.

"Mind your own." Bihan shouldered past, deliberate and challenging, then descended into the pit of sweat and grease that was the brothel's sprawling floor. "Bring him to me. Now. You know I don't wait. Fregor and I will be at the bar."

"W–wait! You can't bring a corpse in—" the eunuch stammered, his thin protest drowned by the band's raucous crescendo.

Bihan carved through the throng. The atmosphere thickened: cheap perfume, sour liquor, unwashed bodies pressed too close. Not only men and women, but gnomes, half-castes, goblins: a menagerie of the city's refuse gathered like flies to *kheghch*. Faces wore either naked greed or abject desperation. Anyone who frequented Felipe Contreras' den was as vile as the man himself, if not worse.

They cheered. They leered. Their eyes fixed on the corpse across Bihan's shoulder, applauding as though it were a bawd's painted smile or a poorly strummed mandolin chord. A fresh kill, they assumed, hungry for spectacle. And they were right. Just not by Bihan's hand. Fregor had always been too quick, too slippery, to die that way. The thought twisted Bihan's gut, a phantom ache knotting behind his eyes. The garnok's strange defiance lingered like a bruise, alongside the question of how it had felled his friend.

Near the stage, an off-key crash of drums grated at him. He eyed the coy drummer, favouring one arm. The rhythm was wrong. Irritating enough to imagine smashing the man's head in. Not today. Not now.

Bihan set Fregor beside him at the bar, the dead man's neck lolling stiffly against the damp wood. He let out a sigh, then another, each drawn from somewhere deeper, heavier. A habit, perhaps, though he no longer knew whether it came from age seeping into his bones or from life's relentless grind gnawing at him. Without a warm bed or gentler comfort to soften the night, the sigh was all he had, a poor man's release, easing the knots in his back and lifting, if only slightly, the press upon his mind.

The bar's bejewelled crown—usually kept proudly beside its amber liquor—was conspicuously absent. Odd. Felipe adored the thing. Bihan turned back to the liquor. He didn't want its name; knowing might sour the rough, numbing burn. Six drinks. That'd always been the order. Six, then five, then four... dwindling companions with every bloody job.

Four dead, one civilian, one adventurer keeping afloat.

Whispers hummed at his side. Magic's re-surfacing. A girl's delicate fingers birthed a flame—impossibly bright, a sprite of pure light. Her pointed ears flushed crimson as her conspirator marvelled. The ashen-haired witch flickered through Bihan's mind, her own long, strange ears marvelled about in the reports from the southern continent. In a shadowed corner, a devil-horned trickster with yellow skin hawked cheap replicas of his kit. Bihan knew the oaken varnish was a fraud; the real artefact the trickster kept for himself.

The guard's heavy boots thudded past. The girl's flame vanished in an instant. The trickster's wares folded away with equal swiftness. As soon as the guard's back turned, both flared back to life. The ritual endured, undeterred by Laic law.

Magic had returned. And the Laics were far from pleased. Mystics—those who wielded such raw power—remained the enemy, feared and hunted like vermin.

"Barman, fetch this man a loincloth and oil him. He doesn't shine enough! Or is it just the light in here? Open those damned curtains!" A man in fine silks preened, chest glistening with sweat, scrawny fingers jingling with gold and silver rings. His cadence dripped with mock sweetness. "What's the matter, Bihan, darling? Not your usual *charming* self?"

Above, the neolyt lamp sputtered, its failing red glow casting jagged shadows across the room. Ember light caught on the key at Bihan's throat, the old metal gleaming with a malevolent spark. Magic and mana could never mingle; a law as absolute as stone, and that perilous truth had seeped into every crevice of the new world. An unseen contagion threading its way through all who lived within it.

Bihan's timbre was flat as he downed his sixth drink, molten liquor burning a sticky path down his throat. "I want my pay. Ten gold, if I recall."

He lifted his gaze to the bar's polished platinum mirror. A pierced nose flattened and marred, lips uneven: an upper thin as a scar-line, a lower too full, too soft. Worst of all, his brow hung low, shadowing the only decent feature: his eyes. His mother's eyes, a lone spark of her lost beauty.

Felipe clapped a delicate hand on his scarred shoulder, trailing sweat and cosmetic residue along the map of old wounds across Bihan's back. A glow flickered faintly behind Felipe's right eye as he launched into his practiced lament: "You'll get your pay when I'm ready. I'm out of pocket this week due to—"

"Today," Bihan cut him off. The word landed like steel. Felipe's head bobbed in quick concession, eyes wide.

Silence rolled outwards, heavy and complete. Bihan's scarred gaze alone was enough to smother the room. He dismissed the barman with a flick of his hand, claimed the bottle of sticky liquor, and extended it towards Felipe. The pimp shrank from the gesture, his ring-laden fingers fluttering in refusal, restless as startled birds.

"Thanks for handling that garnok," Felipe said, twisting his jewellery. "Did you find the dinero he took?" Bihan shook his head. Felipe's laugh came high-pitched, squeaky as scrubbed stone. "He bled me dry. Could've lined your pockets too. Not that I won't, of course. I even took it to the authorities. Where's the justice?"

Bihan drank deep, warmth absent from his words. "The underbelly isn't authority. Likely they hired the garnok, given his reputation… and yours. Best you don't use the word 'justice,' Felipe. You'll sound like a hypocrite. Now tell me how the garnok slipped in here."

Felipe leant closer, conspiratorial. "Simple. Tucked his scaly tail, pulled on a cowl, kept his head low. Looked a bit like you after a bender."

Bihan's brow lifted as he studied the pimp. "Whatever. Pay me. Then I'm gone."

Felipe tugged a small purse from his sash, the coins within jingling a hollow song, and slid it across the bar. With it came a sly smile and an offer to spend the night wrapped in his "finest silks"—the threadbare sheets of the brothel, perfumed with sweat and stale musk. Bihan rolled the purse in his palm, testing its weight, before tucking it into his sporran.

"I'll not squander coin on your gaudy squalor," Bihan said. "I'll rest at the teahouse."

"But the women there… long, ugly toes," Felipe purred, feigning sympathy.

"I don't care." Bihan rose, tossed the bottle into the sawdust, and belched loud enough to stir the rafters.

"You can't deny it," Felipe pressed, his pitch edged with panic. "My offer, I mean."

"I can, and I will." Bihan moved for the door, his shadow stretching long across the warped floorboards. "Goodbye, Felipe."

"Wait! One request. For old times' sake."

Bihan's hand settled heavy on Fregor's shoulder. A sigh worked through him, rough and reluctant. Around them the crowd leant in, a hush swelling like the intake before a song.

Felipe fell to a whisper, slick with theatre. "Do this, and I'll pay for Fregor's rites. A proper send-off for your mate."

Bihan lingered. The offer dangled between them like bait. His gaze slipped from Felipe's greedy eyes to Fregor's slack form: feet bare and dulled with dust, toes curled faintly as though still gripping the earth, while his hands lay open and stilled, once deft enough to lift a purse or coax music from a string. The feet spoke of the grave, nameless and unmarked; the hands of the life lost, quick and clever, now emptied of all purpose. The vision of them lowered into a pauper's pit soured his tongue. His jaw tightened, teeth grinding, as silence thickened around him.

At last, his shoulders sagged. "Five minutes, Felipe. No more. Then I'm gone."

With a desperation verging on panic, Felipe spun a tangled tale of love, intrigue, and reckless adventure. His niece, he claimed, had slipped from his "watchful" eye into the harsh wilds of Enkhara, chasing a quest to rival Bihan's own exploits—perhaps even greater. A grand challenge, a chance to carve her name into the world.

As the barbarian hunched over the bar, his gaze straying to Fregor's unseeing eyes, a familiar tingling crept into his fingertips and toes. Camila hadn't run just anywhere. He sensed she'd gone to Syrek—or what remained of it. The ruin where he'd won the grim, heavy title of Hero, alongside the less flattering names that clung to him.

Felipe's concern was never for her. His true fear gnawed at reputation; word would spread that he'd failed to shield his own kin, and his standing would sink deeper than any whispered ghost tale. He feigned dread of his sister's spirit clawing her way out of the Hells to torment him for losing her daughter, but Bihan knew better. In life the woman had loathed him—his pointy nose, his preening airs—and death wouldn't have softened her spite. She'd no reason to rise from the pit for him, not ever.

The tingling in his fingers and toes lingered, as it had since the southern sundering first tore the world apart. Whether curse, magic, or nothing more than flesh's betrayal, he could never tell. Yet it'd never steered him false. And whenever he thought of the garnok's knowing smile, a chill threaded down his spine. Threads wove together, a dark pattern forming.

Bihan's stomach growled as a meal was set before him: a thin pea broth, its surface broken by sodden lumps of carrot, with a heel of bread so dry it crumbled at his touch. Felipe, ever the miser, had spared no coin for meat or salt, and hunger gnawed sharper for it. Bihan loathed soup in any form, colour, or flavour, yet it was not the bowl he despised most, but the man across from him—Felipe, with his pinched smile and miser's heart—whom he hated with a cold and steady intensity.

"Don't mention my name," Felipe hissed theatrically. "No whispers, no hints. Ask of her around the city, whistle if you must—though she hated my whistling."

Bihan's tone was flat. "What's her name?"

Before Felipe could answer, the barman—always listening—cut in. "Camila Callo, isn't it?"

Felipe puffed. "Camila Callo Contreras. Two surnames, greedy little twat. She uses her mother Delphine's as well."

"Left about a month ago," the barman added, smirking before Bihan's frown wiped it away. "Spoke of sceptres and riches. Said she'd rule Aledhyn with the crown she stole."

Felipe glared at the empty shelf where the bejewelled crown had sat. "Delusions. She was obsessed with you, Bihan. Drew your portraits in her spare hours. Watched you from the staircase—that one over there. Always watching."

Bihan scowled. "I never noticed."

"You'd have liked her," Felipe insisted, slurping his thin soup. "Dirty-blonde hair, golden skin, breasts to make a priest blush, hazel eyes—one flecked with blue—and small, dainty feet. Not like those trotters at the teahouse."

"Did she take supplies?" Bihan asked, cutting through the sleaze.

"Enough for a fortnight, maybe," the barman said. "Took coin too. She's been saving."

"Stealing," Felipe snapped. "Nearly lost her hand robbing a Seaborne merchant's purse—"

"Enough." Bihan's voice cracked the air, silencing both. "First-timers squander every scrap. Did she take gold?"

"A dozen, maybe fifteen coins," said the barman.

Foolish. Any seasoned thief would've broken it down into silver and copper, harder to lose, harder to steal. Bihan rose, pacing, his footsteps heavy on the warped boards.

"Gold's a beacon," he muttered. "Silver and copper keep most knives at bay, unless desperation drives them."

Felipe frowned. "Why's that?"

Bihan smirked, leaving the secrets unspoken. He thought of polished scabbards and scuffed ones, how they marked novices and killers alike. Knowledge better left unsaid. A master thief gauging risk against reward.

As he circled the bar, something warm stirred low within him, a glow he'd almost forgotten. Camila's quiet devotion didn't repulse; it tugged at a memory of Alihan Hammerfist, who once lit that same fire in him. He could almost taste her hunger for legacy, a yearning to carve her name into stone as lasting as his father's broken blade.

For too many years he'd trudged through life with nothing but boredom for company, despair shadowing his steps. Now a flicker rose in his chest, fragile yet fierce, perilously close to excitement. Even the familiar tingling in his fingers and toes, that omen he could never name, curled through him not with dread but with the edge of a grin.

Bihan the Beauty let himself lean into the promise of another road. He remembered when such callings still outshone weariness, when adventure was not a burden but a breath. Perhaps one more journey could coax that spark into flame.

But first came Fregor. Not a tavern pit, not the rot of saw-dust and forgotten bones. A grave. A stone. A rite. After that, he would find a companion—another soul to share the miles and the hazards. He already knew where to begin: above ground and in the heart of the Circular City.

II

The Scent of Mourning Silk

He left that same night to bury his friend. The city's nocturnal hum drifted like a faraway echo beneath his measured steps. Felipe honoured his promise to cover the costs, though every coin parted from his hand seemed to carve reluctance into his features. By starlight, two weary labourers dug the grave, their shovels rasping through earth as soft as ash. At its head they set a plain marker, no Reaper motif, humble and near-anonymous among the cemetery's weathered effigies.

It wasn't the sweeping sea view Bihan had once dreamt for Fregor. Yet from this modest rise he caught a glimpse of the bay, twilight rippling across its surface, while strings of laundry hung from balcony lines, banners of colour swaying against the night. There was a quiet, melancholy beauty here.

Less grand than they'd once imagined, yet poignant in its simplicity.

Bihan pressed his lips into a hard line as he stood among leaning stones and worn carvings, the only sound the distant, uneven lilt of the city. He was a man of action, not words, and now, over soil newly turned and rich with iron and clay, he found no speech within him. The cheap stone bore only GREGORY THE NUTPURSE. The name scored hastily and incorrectly by an unskilled hand.

All their shared adventures—raised glasses, raucous feasts, whispered confidences—flooded the silence of his mind, leaving only a cavernous ache in their wake. No tears came; the well had long since run dry. Instead, absence pressed down on him, relentless, where grief should've flowed.

Finality came not with the chisel, but with the slow descent of the coffin. Inch by inch, the rough wood slipped into the earth's cold embrace. The moment it vanished, a blow struck his ribs, robbing him of breath. Fregor was gone, swallowed by soil, never to return. Bihan reached out without thought, his calloused hand settling on the cool stone. He stood unmoving as the stars above needled through the velvet sky, remembering the trivial and the momentous alike: the quiet vigils, the small, mundane rituals that now glowed in memory with a sudden, aching splendour.

Then movement caught the edge of his vision: a slender enrobed woman cloaked in shadow, a boy beside her, both still as sentinels. They lingered at a respectful distance, watching. Without turning, Bihan sank against the back of the tombstone, its rough chill propping his weary frame. He rested his head against the stone and sighed; the sound lost to the hush that ruled the graves.

He remained until dawn, a lone sentinel beside his friend. When the eastern sky bloomed rose and gold and the roosters' raucous crow split the stillness, Bihan the Beauty hadn't moved, bound to the earth by a silent promise.

Brushing the damp earth from his kilt, Bihan set his course for the northern sūq just beyond Aledhyn's walls.

Banks wouldn't open until near midday, leaving him a stretch of idle hours that felt strangely adrift. His purpose was twofold: to discover which bank Rabia had wormed her way into, and to taste the pomegranates he remembered as the sweetest in the world. Scarlet seeds he'd once spat like raindrops in childish games, each ruby kernel a tether to a simpler past, untainted by blood and intrigue.

Felipe had only shrugged when pressed for her whereabouts. The bordello's barman and its hulking eunuch guardsmen wore identical masks of ignorance, equal parts evasion and apathy. If anyone knew, it would be the merchants of the sūq, where gossip rose and curled through every stall like incense smoke.

The northern market pulled at him in ways the rest of Aledhyn never could. Its clamour was raw, untamed, stripped of the rehearsed pomp that cloaked other quarters. Here, a man could vanish in the tide of bodies without trace, carried off by the surge of barter. Here, too, memory lingered: Rabia at his side in reckless youth, laughter sharp as the crack of stolen fruit, pomegranate juice running down their chins, the stain of guilt gleaming on their mouths brighter than confession.

The stones beneath his sandals seemed to murmur forgotten tales, the archdiocese spire cast its long shadow across the square, and at the centre the fountain shimmered like a relic of older ages. Hexagonal mosaics unfurled from its base like ripples in stone, while statuettes of heroes ringed the pedestal, each figure straining skywards to bear its peak. Their stature was no accident—giants for great deeds, lesser forms for smaller triumphs—an architecture of legacy, pressed into water and stone, encircled by stalls that spiralled outwards as though the city itself had grown from that sacred heart.

To Bihan, the sūq was civilisation's heartbeat: unruly, unashamed, alive. Here, weariness ebbed, purpose surged. For the first time in months the road ahead looked clear, almost laughably so: find Rabia, bind her to his cause, then follow the trail of the girl Camila Callo Contreras.

He threaded through the lanes, past eastern merchants murmuring reverence over idols of the murdered Empress, past the familiar devil-horned trickster whispering his hollow cantrips as he hardened the varnish on his false kits. The spell left its mark on the air: the scent of burning timber dampened by rain, laced with a faint spice of cinnamon. Rimatheans hawked jars of "magical" red soil from the fabled Falls Creek; charlatans offered dyed hair, swearing it was plucked from the ashen-haired witch herself. Enkharans spread silks that rippled like flowing water, spices keen enough to sting the eyes, and phials of rare alchemy glittering in the light.

None spoke Rabia's name.

His old pomegranate seller, weary-eyed and stoop-backed, pressed a swollen fruit into Bihan's hand, not in thanks but in apology, a mute concession for the truth he wouldn't voice. A flicker of guilt crossed the old man's eyes before he turned away, as if saying Rabia's name was taboo. Bihan cracked the fruit open, seeds spilling like bloodied jewels, and smirked, a rare and genuine curve of his lips, as the chorus of merchants swelled. Rivals lifted their cries in unison, their voices braiding into a tide of commerce that battered every passer-by. None could withstand the din, whether they sought a silken scarf or a pickled toad's tongue.

Bihan tested the rhythm with a turbaned seller whose braided silver beard brushed his belt, trading laughter until Rabia's name slipped into the air. The man's smile withered; he thumbed his nose in superstitious contempt. Nearby, a silk-shawled woman bent over a customer's foot, small and honey-brown, the skin dusted from the street yet softened by care. Her brush traced delicate whorls of henna across the toes, each curve a fleeting art destined to fade. Bihan's eyes lingered a moment longer than they should've before he mentioned the khorvo banker and she glanced up, her expression hardening.

She spat at his sandals in wordless dismissal, and with a curl of his lip he flicked his last pomegranate seeds at her, a childish but satisfying defiance.

Bankers were hated everywhere, yet Rabia endured as legend: a paradox who could charm sorcerers when desperation demanded, a woman shaped in the age when magic's wild pulse hadn't yet been shackled. Still, the market bristled at her name.

Running low on options, Bihan set a gleaming gold coin on a tottering pile of copper and silver on a grubby table. The scrawny man behind it raised a thin, trembling finger and traced the path ahead. A lead, of sorts. Bihan mistrusted such fingers, all bone and jitter, but with only nine gold left in his sporran he let the risk stand.

The trail bent into a half-ring of steep steps, each rising towards a door as narrow and unassuming as its neighbour. Middle-class flats huddled shoulder to shoulder, their thresholds fractured by twisting alleys that spiralled deeper into the inner precincts of burnished walls and fluttering imperial banners. Which way led beyond the inner-city ramparts? The bony finger had indicated with more hesitation than certainty, a promise that felt as brittle as dry twigs underfoot.

Instinct whispered right. It always had. Decades of alleyway chases and battlefield charges thrummed in his bones, and he heeded them now. He strode into the curve with confidence, only to be engulfed by a chorus of shrill, squeaking voices, and a dozen grubby hands clawing for his kilt pin.

Guttersnipe rogues. His jaw tightened.

Tiny fingers plucked at his scabbards, tugged at his ear-rings. A few even sprang upwards and against his hair like spring-loaded devils. Their cries tangled together in a maddening chorus: "Join Toussaint's army! Retake the Imperium! Al-Qiyamah!" one piped. Another bargained, "Winsome mother for sale—two gold coins, no more!"

"Enough." Bihan's growl rumbled like distant thunder, sweeping through the alley and scattering the swarm in a single arc of his arms. They stumbled across the cobbles, skidding to a halt at the sight of the coin he pressed into view, its dull burnished gleam igniting a feral glint in their eyes. He slid a second piece alongside the first, a sleight of hand that might've been witchcraft to children drunk on hunger. "Take me to Rabia," he said, letting the coins clink, "and these are yours."

The alley erupted. Fists flew, elbows jabbed, teeth sank into flesh. Dust rose in a frenzy of snarls and shrieks, a storm of desperation. Only one boy held back—the same who'd tried hawking his mother's charms. He threaded through the scuffle untouched, then matched Bihan's stride. His silent nod angled right. Bihan let out a rough chuckle. Always the right.

"Follow me, sir." The boy's tone was too steady for his years. He eyed Bihan's arms. "Strong man. Killer, yes?"

"A killer of beasts and men," Bihan rumbled, a half-smile tugging at his lips. "At least, if tavern tongues speak true, or if the bards haven't gilded their stories too much."

The boy puffed his chest and flexed a reed-thin arm. "Mine are bigger."

"Yeah. Maybe one day." Bihan's laugh rumbled against the stones. "Rabia, then?"

"Yes. This way." The boy sighed as though burdened, then waved him on.

They pressed on through a gauntlet of winding alleys, walls rough with ancient mortar and jutting nails rusted to a needle point. One caught Bihan's shoulder, drawing a faint sting, and his gaze flicked to a flapping recruitment poster. Bold, brash letters screamed: DON'T BE DAFT, ACCEPT THE DRAFT! Beneath, in cramped, almost apologetic print, the promise of a hidden contract: hunting basalt stelae for the throneless imperator. The reward could buy him a life of quiet anonymity, but only by stepping into a peril that might shred the soul to ribbons.

"Come," the child urged, seizing one of Bihan's vast fingers in his grubby fist. "Not far."

They broke suddenly into a sun-washed piazza. Concubines reclined in filigreed gazebos, feeding patrons grapes with lacquered, precise fingers, their laughter fluttering like birdsong. Artists bent over pale canvases, capturing curves too generous to be restrained by mere brushwork. One lay on her stomach, golden skin gleaming in the light, pillowy breasts pressed against the cloth beneath her, hips rounding in a languid arc, and soles scrunched and lifted behind her like soft, delicate ornaments. Bihan's chest tightened, a flicker of heat threading through him as he drank in the sensual artistry without shame.

Mandolins trilled from sun-drenched balconies while taxmen clicked polished boots across the stones. Here, the clamour of the outer city vanished, smothered by birdsong, preening politicians, and the careful, powdered order of a world untouched by street grime.

At its centre loomed Belmont Bank, a fortress of baroque arches crowned with a slender windcatcher, stone chiselled in the austere, modern grace of Enkhara's north. Olive branches flanked the doorway, their leaves brushing the threshold in a whisper of green. Guards stood at attention, rapiers and flintlocks glinting at their hips, more ornament than threat, catching the sunlight like burnished promises.

Bihan flicked a coin to the boy's shoes. "Off with you."

The child pocketed it and slouched against Belmont's doors, peeling off his purple, star-spangled fez to reveal greasy brunette hair streaked with grey.

"Friends," he declared, voice small but confident, a grin too knowing for someone so young curling across his face like a shadow that didn't quite belong.

Bihan scowled. "No. I've no friends. Not anymore. Bugger off, boy."

"Protection's good dinero," the guttersnipe replied smoothly. "And you owe me two. You showed two."

"I lied. Thieves do that." Bihan's growl rumbled deep in his chest, a low warning that carried more weight than words. Yet those light-violet eyes met his gaze, glimmering with the quiet fatigue of someone far older. "Go before I finish my business, or I'll be angry."

Threats meant little to a child like this, Bihan knew, yet letting the frustration slip free offered a rare, satisfying release. With only eight gold coins to his name, frugality was essential; the boy would tire soon enough. He left the brat to his grin and pushed open the iron doors. The hinges groaned like old bones, protesting the intrusion. A cool breath of air swept over his damp neck, fragrant with orange blossom, sharp rosemary, simmering tomato paste, and beneath it all, the metallic tang of coin. Rabia. Her presence lingered in the space, as tangible as dust motes quivering in the sunlight.

His sandals whispered against the marble, each step a soft, hissing caress, as though the stone itself conspired with memory. A smirk tugged at his lips. The foyer was austere yet intimate: a single pot plant clung stubbornly to life, a velvet settee sank into shadow, and a grandfather clock ticked with obsessive rhythm, measuring time as though it feared arriving late for Rabia: the rogue turned banker.

Bihan paused on the mosaic 'B' set into the centre of the floor. Behind the bars squatted a porcine woman, her slack lips glistening with spittle, chin tucked into a double fold of jowl. She crooked a fat finger with the weary, pompous authority of someone convinced the world existed solely to serve her displeasure. Every movement was deliberate, ponderous, and contemptuous. She rarely moved, and only to punctuate her judgement, each gestation dripping with the tedious certitude of entitlement.

Above her desk hung the iron fist of Toussaint, the dethroned imperator. The old crest, dusted off for rebellion. The sight tightened something in Bihan's chest. Every uprising wore the same mask in the end: tyranny by a new name. Yet people clung to banners like children to blankets, blind to the wolves waiting in the folds of cloth and hope.

"Here to pledge fealty to Imperator Toussaint?" the teller rasped, her slack lips parting in a grin that gleamed with unwarranted authority. "Face like yours suits the part."

Bihan let a chuckle rumble through him, thumb brushing Alihan's broken blade at his hip. "I'd sooner pledge to a warm bed and a full meal. I'm here for Rabia."

She leant forwards, and a fine spray caught the light, shimmering on the grey wisps above her lip. "I'm afraid there's no one here by that name. Apologies. Now, please, see yourself out. We've pressing matters to attend to."

Bihan stepped closer, sandals hissing against the marble, each soft whisper a quiet assertion. "Her scent lingers here. Faint but unmistakable. If she's here—and she is—she would've opened an account for me, her trusted friend." His lie landed steady. "Check."

"A 'please' would be nice, barbarian." The woman drew in a long breath and rolled her eyes with theatrical contempt. "Under what name?"

"Alihanson. Or Hammerfist."

"Won't be a moment." Grinding her teeth, she flicked her wrist at the velvet bench. "Wait there. And keep your hands from the dates. They're for pledgers, not ruffians dragged in from the gutter."

The promised "moment" stretched into two long, punishing hours. The bank's cool refuge soured to a biting chill that crept into Bihan's marrow until his shoulders trembled despite himself. He glared at the pot plant, its leaves shivering as if the windcatcher above had been enchanted to test his resolve. Each draught that slid across his skin felt like rebuke, raising a rash of gooseflesh he couldn't quell. Crossing his massive arms, he rubbed at them in slow, frustrated strokes. The grandfather clock tolled in tiny hammers against his skull; each beat magnified into irritation until his patience frayed to threads.

The teller never flinched. She sat fixed behind her iron bars, eyes averted, though sweat gathered on her cratered brow. Her indifference was deliberate, each lazy blink another spark against his temper. He inched forwards on the narrow bench, edging closer to the forbidden bowl of dates as if defiance itself could warm him. When her only reply was a yawn, he seized the lot and stuffed them down with the hunger of spite. The fleeting sweetness only sharpened the ache in his gut.

He had not tasted a true feast since before the garnok. Once, men like him were hailed with salted pork glistening with fat, grapes spilling from silver bowls, and ale poured without end. Now, heroes were fobbed off with lukewarm soup and dry bread, gratitude as hollow as the bowls that carried it. The world, he thought bitterly, had grown mean and thankless.

A snort broke the silence, bouncing bright off marble and brass. Bihan lifted his head. Rabia stood poised at the head of the grand stairwell, framed by gilt arch and shadow. She wore finery that shimmered in restraint, suede slippers flashing like starlight, as her chin quivered with suppressed laughter.

"By my horns!" she cried, her voice alive with mirth. "Do my eyes deceive me, or has the world truly spun off its axis? Surely the Hero of the Syrek War—Birthling of the Skärgon Sept, Bihan the Beauty; the Thebian who tore the horns from my late husband's head—wouldn't be found shivering in a lifeless bank awaiting little old me."

Bihan rose, a smile thawing his hard features, her warmth filling the cavernous space. "I gave you those horns as a gift, Rabia," he said, teeth flashing. "Yet here you are, newly horned, and no longer in need of them. Females don't sprout them, last I checked."

She descended with the same irrepressible flair he remembered, clapping her hands in rhythm, whistling a lilting tune that echoed through the hall. At the foot of the stairs, she offered her hand, mischief and history burning in her beady black eyes. "Like our old general, I'm one of the lucky ones," she said, squeezing firmly. "I've missed you, Bihan. Truly."

"And I you. How fares the back?" His question softened the edge of his tone.

Her wince betrayed the truth before her words came. "Abysmal. Heat stirs it worse than chill—a cruel jest from the fates." Their laughter mingled, warm but hollow in the marble chamber. Then Rabia snapped her gaze to the teller. "Lock the doors. Shut the ledgers. And take down that fist of Toussaint. Al-Qiyamah, my arse."

The teller jolted into motion, sluggish no more, though the crest hung stubborn above her head in silent defiance.

"Rabia," Bihan interjected, "before you lock up, I've gold that needs converting—"

"—into silver and copper. I know your tricks," she cut in, eyes rolling. "But not after hours. You'll dine at mine, meet my wife, and we'll sort your coin in the morning. No arguments, unless you prefer another bank."

"Don't tempt me," Bihan smirked. "Sakogiannis Bank never buried me in theatrics or had me waiting in their cold foyer for hours. Anyway, did you open an account for me?"

"Of course, I..." Her long ears twitched, alert to something beyond him. She darted around his leg and peered towards the iron doors. "Shadi," she murmured, lips curling in fond annoyance. "That little tramp is still out there, clinging to his foolish hope like a limpet." She sniffed the air, bit her blackened lip, and waved him to follow. "Come. I've a back door for pests like him."

Together they slipped through the rear passage, their steps finding the same rhythm as in old campaigns. The broad alley opened towards the medial wall, built wide for carriages and couriers, and they moved with ease through its hush.

Lordlings and nobles turned to gawk as the pair passed: Bihan's towering, scarred bulk beside Rabia's vivid, unpredictable spark. A sight too strange to ignore, a contrast etched into memory and an unforgettable pairing in the staid inner city. In that moment, he realised, with a weight both sharp and welcome, just how much he'd missed her.

III

To Forfeit a Future

Rabia's house stood where the outer city's clamour broke against the medial wall, its noise dimmed to a hush of order beyond. A towering windcatcher crowned the three-storey residence, flaunting Rabia's wealth more surely than any jewel. The walls were raised from the costliest stone, each block cut to a mason's precision, its austere façade betraying nothing of the splendour within.

Through the tall mesquite door, its dark grain steeped with sandalwood whose warmth unfurled like incense, lay a hidden oasis. Marble floors softened by embroidered cushions, lanterns burning amber light, courtyards blooming with secret gardens. Bihan drew the sandalwood deep into his lungs, and with it came Syrek, memories jagged as craggy mountains. A twitch stirred his jaw as grief pressed close, the scars of that land refusing to fade.

The table bent beneath the feast. Platters of molten cheese and spiced meats, saffron rice gleaming with oil, trays of sugared pastries and dates stuffed with nuts. Bihan ate as though starved, hunger stripping away his civility until even he felt the barbarian rawness of it. When at last his belly ached, he leant back with the weary satisfaction of a soldier who'd fought and won. Rabia's wife had been architect of this plenty, her shy smiles and graceful tending outshining Rabia's easy laughter.

That laughter faltered. Mid-story, Rabia clutched her back, her smile thinning to a shadow. Bihan's hand lifted instinctively, then hung in hesitation as she withdrew, offering only a fragile, unreadable half-smile. Her gaze strayed to the wall where twin tomahawks gleamed, relics of deeds never truly buried. Syrek again: massacres, ghosts, and unhealed wounds.

Did Rabia hold him to blame? Or was her silence over Fregor's death a wound too deep to name? She'd spoken of neither, and the absence rang louder than any lament.

A darker unease coiled in him; why had Camila gone to Syrek, of all cursed places? What drew her to the cradle of their nightmares? Did a deeper wound beyond her aching back cause Rabia to disband from their party without farewell?

Servants replenished the table until it seemed bottomless: steaming bowls of lentils, ribs crusted with salt, honeyed dates bursting with syrup, tomatoes dried to scarlet leather and paired with brined feta. Bihan devoured each as though at war with hunger. Around him seven children scrabbled for morsels, laughter bright as cymbals, grubby hands darting between the dishes.

All but the youngest were adopted. The infant, named Bihan, gurgled at the table, his horn-buds pushing through his scalp. The warrior, so often unmoved by children, felt something twist within him at the sight.

Watching their eager hands, their heads bent in quiet devotion to food, his thoughts wandered. A hearth tended through decades, mornings steeped in tea and memory, laughter worn smooth by time until only its echo lingered. Love stitched into chores, hair silvering strand by strand. Was such life possible for him, or had he condemned himself to scorn its calm richness? The thought rang hollow, a lie he'd told too often. For every child's laugh, every couple's embrace, called to something he still longed for, even as he fled it.

Yet the road sang in his blood. Mountains conquered, battles carved into legend, the rush of destiny burning in his chest. Boredom had once crept like fog over him, but Camila Callo's reckless trail had cut through the haze, stoking the fire anew. Her daring had become his compass, and he'd follow it, even into Syrek.

When the third course yielded to quiet satisfaction, Rabia rose and pressed into his hands two porcelain cups of coffee: dark, thick, and rich as earth. She drew him out to the moonlit balcony, granting her wife a reprieve from the clamour.

Behind them the children still fizzed with excitement, too enthralled by the fabled Last Barbarian to yield to sleep.

Moonlight spilt across the balcony. The night air, laced with jasmine and cool stone, brushed Bihan's scarred cheeks like the caress of an old friend. From the minaret, the Muzali call to prayer rose mournful as the moons climbed, silvering the Circular City in gentle light. He unclenched his fist around familiar complaints about crowded streets and sti-fling walls, but tonight the city hummed a different tune, one that beckoned with the promise of roots and stillness.

Rabia set a brass hookah between them, its coals glowing as she coaxed the flame. Handing him the mouthpiece, she lingered in the curl of fragrant smoke. Sweet apple drifted in mint's cool shadow, the same blend Fregor once favoured, the same one Rabia had once scoured the sūq to find. Each breath carried memory and tribute together.

"You've something on your mind, old friend, and it isn't coin or Fregor's death. May the divines guide him home, wherever that may be." Her voice drifted from beneath the low arch of her cushioned nook, where she reclined overlook-ing Belmont Bank. She tucked a strand of dark hair behind her ear, then smirked. "I trust it isn't my wife you're fretting over, barbarian. I've claimed her too fiercely for that."

Bihan braced his forearms on the chilled balustrade. He inhaled the sweet smoke, bowed his head, and let the city's scattered lights—fallen stars across endless streets—steady his thoughts. "What happened, Rabia?" His voice was low, weighted. "Why did you leave us all those years ago?"

She shifted among the cushions, fabric whispering under her. A tremor in her shoulder answered before words could. She drained her coffee in one sharp gulp, then exhaled a veil of mint-blue smoke that cloaked her face. Her chipped nails tapped a restless rhythm on the pillows.

Within that haze, she changed the subject. "Tell me about Thebes," she rasped, humour roughened with wear. "In all our years together, you never once described your homeland, your khanate. What was it truly like?"

Bihan closed his eyes against the smoke. He knew she wouldn't answer, not directly, not about the past. Syrek twisted in his memory, and he winced, cursing the divines for its indelible mark. He studied the ornate mouthpiece instead, the same one he'd carried from the road to Aledhyn, the same path that'd forced him to leave Rabia broken and scarred in a place she once adored. Those memories cut with painful honesty but left no festering wound like some others.

To speak of Thebes—his throat tightened on the thought. He pinched the porcelain cup between scarred fingers. What colour was his mother's hair? For years he'd pictured sunlit blonde, until a memory surfaced of her brushing out dark tangles. Had his father truly been a towering giant, or was that the lie of a child's awe? Tales of Alihan Hammerfist praised cunning and agility, not size. The omission now seemed telling.

"I can't recall it, Rabia," he confessed. "Neither the scents nor the whispers of my khanate. Only death and ruin. Like

Syrek, but worse. I wish I could touch the good memories again, but they're locked behind a barrier I can't breach."

He turned to the Circular City: the northern, eastern, and western gates standing like sentinels, the outer districts stretching beyond their reach. Palm fronds swayed in the faint wind, and on the horizon, he marked the road to Syrek—Camila's last-known path, and his own inevitable one.

A cold longing gripped him. His thumb traced a worn line in the stone, wishing Rabia might join him this time, share the burden he would otherwise bear alone. He sipped the now-lukewarm coffee, its bitterness suiting his mood, then drew deeply from the hookah. The mingled flavours of apple and mint met the coffee's sour warmth, a comfort harsh and sharp, but his alone to savour.

"Memories are only fragments," he said in a low rumble. "Never the whole truth. Not for people like me, whose pasts splinter and fade." He let the words rest in the night before continuing. "I fear war will find us again. This uprising coils like a viper, waiting to strike. 'Al-Qiyamah,' they whisper, when they should be calling for Muam Al-Dyn, the End of Days. Perhaps this fractured world deserves it."

Rabia sat upright, cushions rustling. Her gaze caught his and held, unblinking. Smoke curled from her lips in languid rings. "I know you, barbarian—better than anyone alive, save Fregor, who truly understood that restless soul of yours. You're not one to bare your heart, nor to pray for Muam Al-Dyn." A brow, neatly painted, lifted. "So why open these wounds now? Syrek, and all the rest. Wounds we both tried to bury."

Bihan swallowed. A knot pulled tight in his chest. He wanted to deny her words, to cloak them in grief or fatigue, yet deep down he knew she was right. From the moment he set out to find her, one question had burnt on his tongue, but he'd resigned himself to Rabia's silence concerning Syrek; its unspoken weight a familiar ache.

Now, something else gnawed at him: that he might drag Rabia back into the battles he once tempted her with—coin and danger in equal measure. Such things had no place in her gilded life now. And yet, when he met her eyes, he glimpsed that same spark he remembered from her first descent down the bank stairs. If he asked with true conviction, she wouldn't hesitate.

He didn't crave Muam Al-Dyn. The notion had been clumsy, a half-spoken signpost to a deeper unrest he lacked words for. Eternal nothingness was no reprieve; it was torment. What he sought, he could hardly name. He knew Rabia shared that hunger for peril, that fire which chewed at the soul when starved. But she'd found a tether—her wife's embrace, her children's laughter, the anchorage of hearth and home. She had more to lose now than the fleeting surge of battle.

Bihan, stripped of parents before boyhood's end, dreaded robbing her children—adopted though they were—of a mother's warmth. He wanted them to be spared that void, the very one he'd carried all his life. He wanted Rabia to enjoy the civilian life.

"Bihan." Rabia's tone softened. "If you ache for the past, if those old joys still pull at you, buy a Pocket Globe. It might grant the respite you need."

"A what?" His brow furrowed.

She rose from the cushions, her shoulder brushing his as she leant against the balustrade. "It sounds absurd. I thought so too, until I tried one. A hobgoblin thaumaturge—a magus—crafts them. Tiny globes, no bigger than an orange, holding whole pocket dimensions. You choose the world, or scenario, and pay a gold coin for each year you wish to dwell there. Outside, only minutes pass. Inside, an eternity."

"Let me guess," Bihan muttered, the words rough, "I trade my soul for a dream."

"No, you mule. It costs coin. When its magic runs out, the globe shatters. They look like trinkets; snow globes dressed in gilt and glass. On the base, a warning: *handle with care.*"

"Fine. I'll think on it." His calloused hand rasped across his scarred cheek before he straightened. He couldn't ask her. Not yet. "Thank you for the feast, and the cambio, Rabia. But I've business pressing."

Rabia stepped forwards, barring his way. "Not so fast. You've given me nothing tonight but platitudes and ghosts. That's your armour, I know it well. Yet you came here, to me, for cambio, though you know my queues are hated across the city. No practical reason, then. So, tell me, Bihan. Why are you truly here?"

He exhaled a slow swirl of smoke and snuffed the hookah ember with a single breath. He drained the coffee and set the porcelain cup on the balustrade, its handle pointing towards the road to Syrek and the small memorial that marked its end. "Felipe's niece vanished," he said. "What began as adventure has become disappearance. She never came back." His tone was flat; the fact lay heavy between them.

"You offered your services to him, a mercenary for coin as always?" Rabia asked.

"I offered nothing," Bihan snapped, picking at the calluses on his palms. He stood and told the story without flourish, how he slew the garnok after Fregor fell, his tense parley with Felipe, the riddles at the bar. He'd not, however, invited Rabia to join him, though his eyes betrayed the plea he wouldn't—couldn't—voice.

Rabia scowled. "Felipe's niece? Big deal. He's a scumbag who deserves what he gets. Why risk yourself for his kin while his own hide rots in comfort?"

"What about Camila?" Bihan shot back. "That girl, she sought more than a brothel's walls. She deserved the chance to choose. She deserves saving."

"If she suffers, perhaps then," Rabia said, straightening despite a sharp wince. "You don't know. She may be feasting in silk under marble idols, sleeping safe in an inn, or lost among Toussaint's ranks. In any case, she fares better than a life in Felipe's brothel."

The growl rose in his chest. "Her friends weep for her, Rabia. Regardless of Felipe's depravity, I'll find her. My word, my honour."

"Alone?" Rabia mocked. "Just you and your wits?"

"Of course," he scoffed. "My khopesh and dagger will see me through."

She laughed, the sound sharp and bright. "Then the wit is plainly lacking, as ever. That 'dagger' of yours is a broken heirloom. A trinket you daren't let me hold for fear it'll vanish."

Bihan's lips thinned. "Careful, Rabia."

Her reply landed like a blade honed to a razor's edge. Had he not loved her, he might've cuffed her horned head on the spot, an impulse held back only by the weight of affection. Yet at the name Camila, something in him sparked. This was no spoiled maiden crying for fortune; she was kindred, lit by her own daring. If she thrived among wealthy suitors, so be it; if she nested beneath an innkeeper's roof, that too would be her choice. But if she'd pledged herself to Toussaint, the danger and the promise would drag them both in.

His decision settled like molten iron in a smith's cast. He would uncover her fate.

Rabia watched him, arms on hips, a mischievous flash lighting her pupil like a southern star. "All right," she said slowly, with the certainty of someone who'd already chosen. "I'm coming too. Don't pretend you didn't want this the moment you crossed my threshold."

He drew a ragged breath. "Rabia, no. Your wife, your family, your injury still haunts you."

"It always will, barbarian. It's my constant companion," she said firmly. "My wife may wail and gnash teeth; that's drama I can weather. The children won't notice; they barely see me as it is with the hours I work. Tell me, then: shall I fetch my tomahawks?"

Wearied of pretence, he nodded. Ceremony had no place between them. He laid a heavy hand on her shoulder. "They sit high for a khorvo. If you must, reach for them."

She rolled her eyes. "At least I'm taller than that Syreki prince."

He remembered the fallen youth and, as a quiet pact, set the pin from his kilt beside the hookah. A silver ornament set with a single ruby. Small payment for the wife he invoked that night, a token of trust and a pledge between equals to bring her back safe.

As he gathered his weapons, he glimpsed Rabia lean into her wife's arms. Her wife wept, then turned with a glare that cut him to the bone. The look said plainly, return her safe, or face my wrath.

He should've asked her to stay. He should've borne the burden alone. He should've confessed that his fingertips and toes tingled with foreboding. Instead, he smoothed the uneven pleats of his kilt, tightened the straps at his waist, and stepped into the night.

IV

The Thirst for an Answer

The deserts between Aledhyn and the rest of Enkhara stretched beneath an unforgiving sky, a vast and hungry maw waiting to swallow the unprepared. Here, a traveller didn't simply walk the sands—they wrestled them. Camel hooves sank into the yielding ground with a muted, rhythmic thud, each step a contest of endurance, while the beasts voiced their discontent in guttural grunts. On the horizon, dunes wavered into mirage, sun-metal and amber melting together until the world dissolved into a single, shimmering veil.

To live as one with this expanse, to achieve the desert's rhythm, was a privilege reserved for nomads and caravanners tempered by decades. Their skin wore the dunes' bronze patina, their eyes deciphered the faintest shift of wind, their spirits plaited into the eternal drift of sand. They kept to themselves, aloof and scattered, seldom crossing the roadside shrines that marked their devotion. Encountering one was like glimpsing a phantom. Yet Bihan and Rabia had already found themselves at spear-point twice since leaving Aledhyn.

On Muzali pilgrimage days, nomads demanded offerings, claiming piety as excuse for plunder, their eyes betraying the ritual's hollowness. Most travellers, knife at throat and delirious beneath the desert's blaze, found such sanctity hard to swallow. Bihan had timed their departure to skirt the cycle, but from the wavering haze figures emerged, shemaghs drawn back just enough to catch the glare of hungry eyes—robes revealing recent spoils.

Hands thrust forwards. "Trinkets and coin mean nothing," rasped the leader, his words dry as sand. "Only that which shines the sacred hue."

Bihan set down silver and copper alone. The nomad froze, eyes narrowing at the meagre tribute. With a sneer, he pulled a crown from his belt—Felipe's crown, gaudy and jewelled, unmistakable—and tossed the coins aside as though they scalded his palm. The crown's metal gleamed sun-metal bright. Bihan allowed himself the faintest curl of satisfaction. The trail was true. With a terse nod, the leader waved them on, content with his prize but disgusted by their offer.

That night, they made camp beneath a scatter of palms where the sand held a memory of shade. From the horizon staggered a lone wanderer clad in battered plate. He offered no name, no word of greeting, only hunger staring hollow from his eyes. Rabia, ever generous, pressed food and water into his hands. He devoured both with frantic haste, as if the act itself could prove he still lived, and fell asleep by the embers, armour glinting dully against the dying fire.

At dawn, the man unburdened himself of steel. Piece by piece, each clang on the earth rang like a funeral bell. Tears carved pale lines through the soot on his cheeks. The last plate slid away to reveal a vambrace stamped with Clan Toussaint's iron fist. Beneath it, his gloves clotted with another's blood, dark beneath his nails.

Desperate, he scoured his hands with sand until the skin broke raw, then tried saliva, then pressed his palms into the embers. The hiss of burning flesh carried into the morning air. Only when sinew blackened to ash did he collapse, trembling, his silence a plea for release. Bihan granted it. With one hand he closed the boy's eyes, with the other he drove his dagger home. The end came swift. Barely more than a youth, he'd known no hearth's comfort, only war's hollow promise.

Rabia prised a parchment from the boy's gambeson and read aloud: "Find the stele! Aid your Imperator and restore the Imperium to its former glory. Be rewarded in riches and love. Serve, and be lauded as lords and ladies."

Bihan's brow furrowed. "The *stele*? A poster in the city spoke of stelae. Plural."

"Humans covet my ancestors' relics, whether one or a hundred." Rabia shrugged. "Perhaps the singular is only a symbol. A myth for the restless to cling to." She swung herself into the saddle, chest lifted in mock heraldry and declaimed with mocking flourish: "Behold our redeemed Imperator, risen from exile with basalt stelae, saviour of the Realm!"

Bihan snorted. "Born of dreams, no doubt. A convenient fabrication."

They left the corpse for vultures and carrion beetles, his last testament written in dust. Death's decree, final and unceremonious.

The "shorter road" Bihan once imagined a shortcut proved a scalding odyssey. By midday, they reached a timeworn caravanserai along the Spice Road, a dusty crossroads where the air was thick with spice-dust, damp canvas, and simmering mutton. Inside, troubadours plucked strings by firelight while a knot of fervent Toussaint loyalists huddled in the corner, their heirloom armour far too bright for the dusk.

These idealists were little more than boys, their borrowed steel too large for their narrow shoulders. They polished a crested vambrace—its iron fist identical to the dead youth's—until its mirror sheen caught their own faces, aglow with devotion. With voices hoarse and untested, they chanted *Al-Qiyamah*—the Return. Their conviction shook the rafters as they proclaimed that a stele, or many stelae (depending on who cried loudest), would secure Imperator Toussaint's victory.

The iron fist unites. Never broken. Never conquered.

Bihan watched without flinching. *Faith*, he thought, *could no more bend steel than sand could stop the sun.* Their zeal reminded him of the Vizier's declaration of war: thunder without storm. When Rabia asked what the emblem meant, a boy cried, "A kraken's labyrinth of lies fades before the fist. Unity through strength. Power to the people."

Strength won't translate the Megaran on those stelae.

Bihan's jaw set. He loathed how children of comfort played at war, mistaking bloodshed for a carnival of slogans and banners. He pulled Rabia away, urging silence, yet even outside the caravanserai he could still feel their cries echoing at his back. The shadow of war trailed them.

They left as the loyalists raised ale in drunken farewell, certain they had won over the travellers. A veiled woman, her face hidden beneath a tight hijab, slipped past the gates clutching a rolled carpet, merging with a lone dervish that spun in the dust, a cipher of mysteries the zealots could never touch.

Beyond the walls, the desert reclaimed them. Bihan listened to its dialect: the shifting sibilance of sand, the pitiless glare of the sun. Scents still baffled him—sour resin, bitter stone, carrion on the breeze. Rabia, blessed with a khorvo's keen nose, charted hidden veins of water, leading them to the desert's furtive lifeblood.

That night, beneath a squat shelter of stone and lime, their fire dwindled to embers as a newborn storm screamed beyond the walls. Bihan, disgust rough in his tone, begged Rabia to bottle water "untouched by human greed"—a purity to balance the loyalists' hollow fervour. Then he sank down, listening to the storm's ravenous cry, his thoughts drifting to Syrek's ruins and to Camila's distant hope.

Why would she endure this barren expanse for a fortune that never ripened? His own wealth had always been dredged from crypts and caverns, places where liches whispered in the dark, not from ruins baked by desert suns. She must have dreamt of legend, having swallowed bardic embellishments of his exploits whole. Yet Syrek was no saga—only a tawdry memorial on an empty plain. He coaxed the coals back to life, hands outstretched to their feeble glow.

The wind carried tales of three pyramids to the west—labyrinthine tombs that promised either treasure or quick extinction, their jewel-crowned apex said to outshine any throne. He'd once slipped through one of those pyramids to cut down a millennia-old mummy and trace a basalt stele's inscription. There'd been no stele, though, only rot and dust.

If Toussaint's legions pressed on Aledhyn blind to that western stele, precious time would rot away. But if Camila sought it—if ambition pulled her into that same snare—she might prove more dangerous than any ruin.

A chill prickled his skin, not from the desert night but from the sudden lull of the wind. He knew these "whispers" for what they were: the muttering of his own desires, and possibilities, dressed in mystical jargon by desert seers.

"*Milddyr asnikt!*" Rabia cursed in the old Megaran tongue, fist pounding the rock. She arched her back, body rebelling against the hard ground—a cruel exchange for the silken chamber she'd left behind.

Bihan leant into the stone mound, tracing the southern constellations as they flickered through veils of sand. Their mute beckon pulled at him southwards to a golden ruin, perhaps, or back to Aledhyn's gates. He wanted neither to return to Syrek nor to unravel the world's riddles alone. He exhaled, curled into himself, and fell asleep.

Bihan woke beneath a slate sky, the storm spent. A ring of palms broke the horizon, their fronds half-green, half-brown, an oasis sprung like a miracle from the desert's ruin. At their feet lay a shallow pool where tadpoles stirred beneath the surface, raindrops tapping a soft tattoo on the water. Cool air washed over him—sweet reprieve after the storm's wrath.

He crouched at the water's edge, scooping its frigid clarity into cupped palms, drinking deeply. Then he emptied Rabia's jar of stormwater and refilled their canteens. Both of them bathed in the pool, shedding the desert's grit before saddling the camels. Even Rabia seemed lighter, her eyes gleaming at the rare mercy of shade and water.

She angled her mount north, towards Syrek's ruins. Bihan swept a hand westwards, to the pyramids. He was opening his mouth to explain why, when the wind spoke first, coiling grains of sand into a perfect column that towered over them. His hand leapt to the hilt of his khopesh. The dust thinned, and in its place stood a stooped figure in tight robes, clutching a bundled roll like a carpet.

A keening squeal drilled into his skull; Rabia flinched, her jaw clenched against the same bone-deep note. Magic.

"Stop, crone," Bihan barked. "Another step and I spill your blood."

The laugh that answered rasped like dry reeds. She hobbled closer, each step birthing fresh shoots by the water's edge. "Warrior, your threats are hollow. Bluster hides fear. I want only your ear, to share the truths you chase in vain."

Her hood fell back. One eye glittered obsidian; the other, blank and pale as snow. A hooked nose curved over moss-green ichor spilling from her lips, dripping to a wart like bristles on her chin. Her robes, though cut fashionably, tugged at a memory he couldn't place.

"Grant me a moment by these waters," she wheezed. "My body groans under a burden. Lend me your attention, and I'll tell you what you crave. Camila, yes? That's her name."

Bihan's grip tightened on his father's broken blade. "I owe you nothing. Speak of her or vanish."

Her grin split her face like a wound. "You'll learn nothing until you kiss me."

"I'll not debase myself for riddles."

She crouched at the lake, her withered fingers skimming its surface. Ripples spread into an image: a blonde woman with henna swirled across hands and feet—ethereal, perfect, and impossibly real. Camila. Bihan's heart hammered. He took an involuntary step closer, lured by her reflection as if drawn into his own promises of adventure that'd inspired her.

His shout cracked the air. "What've you done? Why's she imprisoned?"

Rabia's hand seized his forearm, anchoring him against the Mystic's mirrored waters and dark promise.

The crone rasped, "I'll reveal nothing more until you kiss me. A small price."

Before thought could steady him, Bihan grabbed her narrow waist and pressed his mouth to hers. The shrill keening dissolved. He braced for rot, yet tasted berries and wine, the kiss bafflingly sweet. When he pulled back, breathless with disbelief, the crone was gone. In her place stood a slender woman, sapphire eyes flickering with an otherworldly charm.

Rabia's laughter pealed. "Now I regret not kissing her. Always fortune's darling, aren't you?"

The Mystic smiled, kneeling beside the bundled carpet. "Seaborne," she intoned, voice chiming like hollow glass. "Camila sails on a corsair's ship bound there. Loyalists waylaid her, chasing the same vessel."

Relief loosened Bihan's chest; the dread knot in him eased. If the zealots pursued a ship, they'd turned from the stele—abandoned it, for now. Or so he hoped.

He dropped to his knees. "Was she taken against her will? Is she in danger?"

The woman tilted her head, a smile grazing her lips. With a flick of her wrist, the carpet loosened in a half-unfurl, its folds whispering open. She bent over it, robes sliding high on her thighs, the fabric clinging to her pale, olive skin before surrendering. Slender and long of limb, her figure curved with a quiet defiance of age. Her breasts, uneven beneath the snug fabric, only heightened her strange allure—imperfection lending her a beauty distinct from Camila's golden grace. Not radiant but arresting. A body shaped by hunger, by yearning, by sacrifices uncounted.

Her feet, too long for Bihan's liking, still held a delicate poise. Nails tinted and tended, arches narrow, her step the echo of some forgotten dance. Yet on those feet and climbing her calves ran a lattice of burgundy scars, branded like living runes, each mark whispering of pain endured and bargains struck. The same burns webbed across her slender hands, a map of her pact with magic. The crone's mask had fallen away, leaving the truth of her flesh: a Mystic who'd gambled beauty and body alike, and who'd wager them again to seize what she desired.

"Perhaps she's a stowaway," the sorceress said, fingers toying with the cold metal of Bihan's key. "Or perhaps she pursues a cause greater than treasure."

Bihan pushed aside her scarred hand. "Is she in danger? A simple yes or no." He rose to his full height as the sun broke the cloud cover, splitting the heavens in pale fire.

Her lips curved in a sly challenge. "I'll tell you, if—"

"No." The growl came low, sharp as iron rasped on stone. "If that's all you'll grant me for the price paid, begone."

At his words the carpet convulsed. From its folds lurched a boy—his fez first, purple and oil-stained, stars stitched into its frayed brim. Bihan's heart struck hard against his ribs. The guttersnipe from Aledhyn stood before them, wide-eyed and grinning as though the desert itself had birthed him. Bihan circled, his thoughts ablaze. How long had she shadowed him? What jest was this?

"You're Shadi's mother?" Rabia cut in, scorn curling her tongue. "You let him scuttle through the gutters, peddling tricks for coin? That accent of his was counterfeit... I knew it." She muttered the last in a venomous whisper.

The sorceress drew herself tall, her hand combing through the boy's tangled hair. "He thrives on mischief and freedom. And call him Shadimtha, never Shadi."

"Why drag him here?" Bihan's eyes narrowed to coals. "Why bind his fate to mine, crone?"

"I'm no crone," she hissed, the words reverberating like steel struck in a cavern. "I'm a sorceress."

She clapped once. The air quivered, though nothing seemed to stir. Bihan's gaze slid to her sleeve, where a slender wand coiled like a serpent against hidden scars. She drew it forth, whispered an ancient word, and the boy's body blurred. Bones groaned as they stretched, flesh reshaping with an unsettling grace. Child melted into youth, the mirage collapsing like melted snow.

"A sorcerer in his own right, and a good man," she murmured, pinching the older Shadimtha's cheek. "My son is no hero destined for glory. His one true purpose is to accompany you in a singular quest." Her sapphire gaze bore into Bihan, daring him to refuse.

Bihan studied the youth: shoulders too narrow for a blade, hair already streaked with grey though his years were scarcely twenty, and those rare violet eyes set like jewels beneath dark lashes. In his spindly hand he clutched a black glass marble swaddled in damp, fraying parchment.

"You speak with the confidence of prophets," Bihan said. "Yet visions are only hollow omens dressed in a mystic's tongue, *crone*."

"*Sorceress*," she spat, her teeth bared. Anger burnt like a furnace behind her gaze. "And what if what I glimpsed was true? What if what I glimpsed was the future?"

"Then find yourself a dreamcatcher," he retorted, mounting his camel with a grunt. Rabia swung up after, her grip steady on the reins. "I'll take him as my ward, in exchange for your scrap of news about Camila. Should he fall, the debt is yours to bear, and mine to settle."

Her lips twisted. "Harm him and I'll hunt you through sand and storm. I'll vow vengeance by all I hold sacred."

Bihan's hand tightened round the hilt of his dagger. "That's your right as a mother." He inclined his head, and Rabia reached down, easing the boy into place on her saddle.

"Consider yourself marked, barbarian," the sorceress hissed, her words weighted with curse and prayer alike. "Return him to me whole and unharmed."

"At my side or in a casket," Bihan growled. "He returns, if that's his will."

Her shoulders sagged. A single tear, bright as fractured crystal, traced her cheek. The camels turned southwards, hooves thudding on damp sand. Shadimtha clutched the marble and parchment to his chest, eyes fixed on horizons unknown. Bihan drew a long breath, grit stinging his teeth.

Seaborne beckoned, but first... they needed a ship.

*****

From the moment they left Shadi's mother beneath the swaying palms, the boy's chatter surged, relentless as a desert storm. He spilt forth his ambitions in a torrent. Dreams of mastering necromancy, of apprenticing beneath the reclusive, ashen-haired Mystic who'd rekindled magic in the world, and more. Each boast burnt hot, only to gutter into another, brighter flame: no destiny too vast, no secret beyond his reach.

Bihan endured it in silence, his skull throbbing with each new proclamation. Peace, the one luxury he craved, crumbled beneath the boy's voice. When Shadi at last proclaimed, with solemn certainty, that horses far outstripped camels—fleet, tireless, noble—while camels were lumbering beasts liable to collapse without warning, Bihan's patience cracked. As penance for maligning the humpbacks, he forced the boy to trot alongside Rabia's camel until the creature, with a disdainful snort, consented to tolerate him again.

By the third dawn, Shadi's proclamation proved plain truth. Their camels collapsed, breathless and spent. They made camp among the dunes, but the mounts wouldn't rise the next morning; Bihan and Rabia trudged off on foot, their spoor a tired curse in the sand. Shadi grinned through it all, until a gypsy caravan traded them two rangy horses. Bihan's retribution resumed: the boy marched again at Rabia's mount's pace, shame and penance braided together.

Penniless, after the gypsy had grossly overcharged them and Shadi's mother had pocketed the coin from Aledhyn, Bihan dreaded their return to the city. He swallowed curses and clung to a raw hope: that the fallen boy-warrior's armour still lay whole and would fetch enough to buy them passage to Seaborne. On the fifth day they found him. What remained of flesh clung brittle to bleached bone; vultures had plucked his sockets empty and carrion beetles had stripped sinew to the marrow. His dreams lay scattered to the wind. Still, beneath a fresh drift, his greaves and helm slept unmarred.

Bihan exhaled, a shaky relief, and knelt to reclaim the iron that might buy their crossing.

On the sixth day Aledhyn's circular skyline rose as a bleared smudge on the horizon. They camped by a rusted pumpjack gouging at subterranean wyrm oil, its piston a monotonous heartbeat beneath a starless dome. Hunger gnawed their bellies; rations and water had been sapped by nomads demanding golden tithes, settling on their rations when salvaged armour proved too cumbersome to wrest from a desperate hand. Bihan scolded himself for distraction: Shadi's endless prattle had him overlook another coveted Muzali day. He counted himself fortunate they still had horses.

Hunger and thirst drove Shadi to action. Against Bihan's warning he recalled the old lessons of High Mage Montero and set his will to conjure water and an apple apiece. Rabia pressed her tomahawks together with silent encouragement as the pumpjack's screech grated their nerves. They stood on loose sand, territory for creatures that despised surface magic, each heartbeat loud in the hush before the act. First, liquid sparkled into their canteens, cool and smelling faintly of damp timber and cinnamon. Shadi pumped a triumphant fist; Rabia slapped his back in approval. Bihan watched the tremor underfoot and felt the desert answer.

The dunes didn't merely shift; they writhed. Fire and blanket vanished into a moving mound as grains crawled like living things. The sand split and the beast rose: metasoma of scorpion, body of lion, face of man. Eight hairy, chitinous legs scrubbed the earth; one single red eye burnt like coals, the other a golden stone that flickered with ancient currents. A breath of sulphur rolled from it in slow waves.

Bihan snarled, angling downwind. "Your casting brought this wretch to us, gnat. A manticore. I warned you: no conjuring." His mare reared as he reined in, knuckles whitening on the haft of his khopesh.

"Go easy on the boy, Bihan," Rabia breathed, her voice raw. "We both share this blame."

He handed the reins to her and forsook the long blade for the dagger at his hip; speed and venom would make the khopesh unwieldy. The manticore's metasoma arched high, a black-green drop trembling at the tip. It yawned, needle-sharp teeth flashing. Breath, foul as rot, cut at Bihan's nostrils. Beast and warrior measured each other: a single, loaded heartbeat.

When the creature spoke, its voice uncoiled like a death-rattle across the plain. "Sheathe your blade and explain," it intoned, enunciations curling through the night. "If you raise steel, you will all perish."

Its words snagged on half-remembered lore—his father's lessons about such abominations. Once, in ages past, these creatures answered the summoning of magic.

Bihan lowered his dagger. He knew the beast's threat was no bluff; even a grazing strike from its poisoned barb would doom them. Alone, he might've dared it. Tonight, he wouldn't risk his companions for pride.

Before he could speak, Shadi's voice broke the silence. "My meddling called you here."

The manticore's head tilted, its eyes closing as though drinking from the twin moons. "Who, then, is my summoner? Speak your name. Loudly." Shadi's hand shook around the black marble sphere. Silence stretched. The creature spat. "Coward. Time betrays your kind. A pity."

Bihan stepped forwards, palms raised. "If you refuse the boy as master, what must we give so you return beneath the sands and trouble us no more?"

"Return unserved? Bold words. But I make no such promise." The manticore's gaze slid to the droning pumpjack. "I demand tribute from my summoner. Half a sense, at least."

Shadi swaddled the marble in its damp parchment, his eyes wide with terror. Bihan's frown deepened. He knew this rite: creatures of old demanded sacrifice drawn from their summoner's flesh for reasons like this. The manticore's nod confirmed it. With steady resolve, Bihan lifted his scarred hand to his dimmed left eye—the one half-blinded by a hundred battles. Bones cracked. Nerves screamed. He exhaled through clenched teeth, and flesh gave way. Blood salted the sand as he tore the fleshy orb from its socket. The world tilted sideways.

"Here," he rasped, dry and hoarse. "Take it, and leave."

Pain lanced him like lightning. He collapsed to his knees. Behind him, Rabia spun tales of his heroism, hailing Bihan the Beauty who bartered with a manticore more magnificent still. He knew her words were no idle praise but a coaxing for the ancient thing to accept a Laic's sacrifice. Dawn crept pale across the dunes, gilding the creature's carapace as it lowered its massive head.

"Very well," it intoned, its golden eye whirring like a gear. "But heed me. Should chance or sorcery cross our paths again, I'll exact a toll beyond this token. In plain terms: if ever I lay eyes on you again, only death will settle the debt."

With a quake that shuddered through the desert, the lion's body and spider legs sank into shifting dunes, its aculeus the last to vanish. Somewhere in the drift, Shadi knelt beside the spent barbarian, clutching the marble—its fuchsia iris gleaming like a vow. Copper coated Bihan's tongue as he tasted the cost of honour: one stolen eye for the promise of safe passage.

He woke to the stench of his sweat-soaked bedroll and a headache like a hammer driving shards into his skull. His limbs lay heavy, his breath rasped in a parched throat, pinning him to the sand as the sun blazed overhead. Rabia leant close, her accent soft as sifted sand, telling him he'd lain insensate for a day and a half. Shadi pressed a cloth of conjured water to his cracked lips. Bihan said nothing, only fixed the boy with a glare so cold he flinched.

Slowly, he raised a hand to his ruined socket. Where bone and flesh once met, he found instead a smooth, cool orb thrumming with faint magic. Dreading his reflection, he asked for a mirror. Rabia gave him a tomahawk, its polished steel clearer than any mirror. The blade showed him scars branching raw from brow to cheekbone, fresh and weeping. Nestled in the hollow socket lay the gift: a perfect sphere of darkness, an iris of glowing fuchsia at its heart. No pupil, no warmth, only an unblinking stare.

He groaned low, letting pain surge and ebb as he sank back into coarse sand. At least, he thought, the floaters that once swam across his vision were gone. Small mercy, in a life of crueller trials. A ghost of a grin flickered across his bruised face before oblivion closed its fist again.

V

The Price of Passage

The quay outside Aledhyn's southern gate thronged with novice warriors. Men and women of every shape wriggled into ill-fitting plate and mail, clutching swords and axes either too heavy for their arms or too slight for their pride. Lanterns swung from the towering masts, their glow sliding across rust-flecked cuirasses. Sailors shouted wagers, and bawdy laughter seeped from shadowed doorways where smoke and ale gathered thick as fog. The salty wind soured Bihan's stomach with a mingled tang of sweat, seaweed, and spilt drink—a torment made worse by the marble eye he'd yet to master.

Among the green recruits, he seized an opening. From his bundle, he produced the armour stripped from the fallen youth and placed it in Rabia's hands. She mounted the nearest crate as if it were a dais, her voice rising over the din, honeyed and commanding. She spun a tale of a Rimathean champion, his greaves dented by the curse of an ashen-haired witch who'd laid waste to cities; though their names, she insisted with sly vagueness, had slipped her memory. When a sceptical youth dared ask about the helm's dried stains, she swore on her divine—and on their very reputations—that the blood belonged to the witch's brother, slain while quelling the re-surfacing of magic. Magic that pulsed, even now, in the very steel.

A fresh-faced recruit, spellbound by her theatrics, parted with ten gold and thirteen silver for the relics. Coins clinking in their purses, the trio melted from the crowd and found quarters along the quay: a creaking room with four narrow beds for three gold, a luxury amid Toussaint's army swallowing every roof of Aledhyn. Rabia refused her family's hearth, fearing the ache of a familiar mattress would root her to it. Shadi, too, declined his mother's threshold, muttering of terracotta and vineyards, as if such excuses might mask unrest.

That night their lodgings claimed a fourth occupant: a Paladin of Wolvesmire, in pursuit of a missing brother—Mathaeus—and a rare phial, from the Imperium's fallen capital. Cloaked in grey and silence, he sank to his knees in prayer rather than trade words. Yet as his head bowed, Bihan thought the sheathed sword at his side gave off a faint, otherworldly gleam. Neither Bihan nor Shadi dared question him. Rabia, bold as ever, tried to glimpse the fabled armour beneath his cloak and was met only with a smile, sorrowful and polite.

Before dawn the next morning, they bribed a grizzled seaman thirteen silver to point out the ship bound for Seaborne. He spat tobacco into the foam and jabbed his thumb towards the *Delphine*, her cyan sails emblazoned with a pale-smoke shield and a golden fleur-de-lis. A banner whispered to belong to a clan steeped in necromancy. When the old salt hailed the captain and asked about three new crewmen, the man disappeared belowdecks without answer.

From dawn's pale light until dusk bled red across the horizon, they lingered by the gangplank with nothing but the rhythm of waves for company. Rigging creaked. Stevedores hummed shanties as they hauled barrels and nets. Children darted among legs, eager for tales or coins, sometimes both.

Bihan wandered through the knot of recruits bound for Toussaint's armada. He bartered stories for tidings: of plague sweeping the capital, of the late Empress' allies broken, and even her brother—drawn, quartered, and left for crows. Yet none had heard of Camila Callo, nor of anyone who fit her likeness. The only refrain was of loyalists who'd vanished without a trace.

When the last tale waned, Bihan pressed a gold coin into the palm of a gawky youth. The gesture felt as windblown as the tide, but the boy's grin proved earnest enough to justify the waste. Leaning against a stack of crates, Bihan inhaled the brine and wondered whether a barbarian might learn the salt-sprayed life of a sailor. The *Delphine* loomed proud yet weathered: a late-model carrack with a square-rigged main and foremast, a lateen mizzen, and a high, rounded stern crowned by a tumbling aftercastle. Her forecastle and bowsprit bore scars of old skirmishes—splintered beams and frayed hemp, suggesting the ghosts of cannon fire.

As twilight unfurled across the water, Rabia's voice broke the silence. "Shadi, what's your wand made of?" Her legs swung idly over the dock's edge.

"Pearwood," Shadi answered, slipping the folded parchment into his vest. "High Mage Montero's quarterstaff is a true marvel, though. Quartersawn oak, iron inlays from the Infernal Isles, and a bronze spearhead. He let me hold it once."

Rabia arched a brow. "What's he to you, then? Your master?"

Shadi shrugged. "Mother's old friend. A wizard, apparently. Works in Seaborne now."

A flicker of unease passed between Rabia and Bihan. Syrek's fallen Vizier had borne a title near the same, though his ruin lay buried with the city itself. Then came the pain—sudden, searing. The marble in Bihan's skull thrummed against his temples. His grip clutched the crates as his vision fluttered with images not his own: gothic towers rising against a storm, tattoos sparking with wildfire magic, shadows swallowing the sky whole.

Shadi's violet eyes fixed on him. "You all right?"

Bihan tapped the marble eye. The hum coursed through his fingertip like a muted heartbeat. "Lucidity's overrated." He turned to Shadi. "Ground rules. No surprise sorcery. Keep that wand sheathed unless we're staring down a death-dealer."

Shadi nodded, lips pressed thin. Rabia only grinned, untroubled. Bihan studied the boy—his knobby joints, his horizon-wide eyes—and wondered if trust was a coin his people could no longer afford. In the lull before their voyage, he swore both body and mind would be honed to steel for the trials ahead.

Glancing again at Shadi, Bihan felt no spark of kinship—only doubt. Among his own kin, strength was measured in silence, forged through years of discipline, every scar a vow. Shadi bore none of it. Watching him fumble over the parchment, Bihan wondered if the youth could even muster the letters scratched on it.

The captain's booming cadence cut through the dockside clamour. "Sorry to keep you waiting! Let's find some fruit, eh? Too damned hot to stand about."

He was a rotund, swarthy fellow, his sausage-thick fingers stained with grease and pitch. A brown beard shot through with grey framed a gaping cheek wound that bared crooked teeth in perpetual grin. His nose, raw and ruddy, spoke either of drink or of a sun that refused mercy. A tricorn perched jauntily above otherwise modest attire, while twin cyan-stitched baldrics strained across his jiggling belly.

Bihan stepped forwards, offering his forearm. The captain's gaze snagged instead on the black marble eye, and his grin widened. "Not my call. Crew won't trust you three. Sorcerers bring storms. Stout folk slit throats in their sleep. And

Bihan the Beauty with a black stone eye? They say you'll murder us all before the voyage's end."

Bihan's fists curled. "Then we'll find another ship."

"There isn't one." The captain strolled on as though leading a parade. "Toussaint's armada swallows every sail. I'm the last bound for Seaborne this fortnight. Now, calm yourself. I haven't finished. To sail as friends and companions, my crew demands you prove yourselves first."

"Friends? Companions?" Rabia scoffed, her tone sweet with venom. "What's the task, then? Steal a silver fleece? The golden ones are long gone."

The captain plucked an apple from a frail merchant's stall, bit into its flesh, and wiped the juice across his open wound. "They want your horses, aye. But mainly? They want Syreki Chardonnay. Twelve years old, exact."

Bihan caught his sleeve before he could take another bite. "Twelve years? Syreki vineyards burnt in the war. Rabia and I fought in those fields."

"As did I," the captain said, yanking free. "Over twenty years ago, if my memory serves."

"Then you know it's impossible. Why set odds no man can meet? Why twelve years?"

"Because it pairs swimmingly with fish," the captain replied, flicking his wrist in mock grace. "And don't think you'll fool us with counterfeits. We've drunk every imitation under the sun. Only Syreki remains untasted."

Bihan's temper darkened. "Damn your wine! We must reach Seaborne now. Chasing impossibilities is no option."

The tricorn dipped as his lips curled into a sly smile. "Then move your arse, my dear barbarian. Unless you'd rather wait a few years. Word in Aledhyn says someone plans to bring the old city back."

A low growl rumbled from Bihan's chest. Restoring a vanished metropolis was as laughable as finding a perfect dozen-year vintage. Not unless someone had smuggled a vine cutting past Syrek's gothic walls. Rumour told of a lone enrobed thief who'd done just that, though such tales grew taller with every retelling. Besides, grapes wouldn't ripen for months yet. A hidden grower nursing Syreki vines in secret? As unlikely as unearthing the vintage itself.

With a roar, Bihan upended the apple stall, scattering fruit into the bay. When the stallholder wailed, Bihan hurled him in after it, a gold coin ringing off his brow as he splashed. "Sorry," he muttered, counting what remained. Five gold left.

Magic was the last resort. If Shadi could turn water to wine, perhaps he might conjure the vintage. But what of the taste? The colour? Even if they described Syreki Chardonnay's fruity notes of lemon and whispers of vanilla, the subtleties of oak and age would slip beyond him.

Shadi's quiet whisper cut through the storm of Bihan's agitation. "My mother." His eyes flicked towards the sea. "The thief who stole the cutting... she's my mother."

Relief eased the steel in Bihan's chest, dulling the marble's sting in his skull. He remembered the sorceress at the oasis: her wand, her lattice of scars, her illusions. A laugh burst unbidden from him, so loud the captain spun around, blanching before hurrying his pace. Rabia joined in, rich and wicked, while Shadi stood pale as sun-bleached driftwood, whispering "Terracotta" again with a tremor.

Bihan clasped the boy's shoulder, steady as iron. "Lead the way, Shadi. Time's slipping. Take us home. We'll manage the rest."

They carved a silent path through the outer city, skirting the half-ruined casbah to the west—still garrisoned by spearmen in faded regalia—before threading into the dye district. Here the streets shimmered with every hue under the sun: façades washed in cobalt and vermilion, walls engineered to catch both light and the wandering eye. Dyers paused mid-stroke, foreheads grazing Bihan's calves in reverent bows, palms pressed to hearts. They still honoured the echo of some long-forgotten deed which'd elevated his status among them.

As dusk bled into the Circular City, the air thickened with spice. Garlic hissed in saffron oil, cinnamon bark curled into sweetness over flames, and earthy perfumes, untouched by sorcery, rose like hymns from street-corner braziers. Bihan closed his eye, letting the aroma guide him like a compass needle towards Shadi's home in the old quarter beyond the western gate.

This quarter predated all but the round city itself. Hulking brick bastions, their buttresses etched in squared meandros, pressed shoulder-to-shoulder with newer dwellings. Foliate arches blossomed into muqarnas vaults; interlaced spandrels winked with torchlight; geometry spun into living scripture. Bihan lingered, breathing in the mathematics of stone.

From the thrum of rival pottery stalls stepped a barrel merchant, pale as unglazed clay. Her silver-grey eyes, one softly glowing, snared him. Silk of muted rose clung to her shoulders; beneath, a charcoal braid fell to her hips. When Rabia asked about the tawny mapwork across her hand, the woman traced its edge. Vitiligo, she whispered—a plague's ruin, a lineage undone. But to Bihan it was beauty painted against uniformity, fragility made defiant.

Two gold coins pressed into her trembling palm bought a modest oak barrel worth less than firewood. She wept relief, and though absurdly overpriced, it was enough. Sailors would scoff at bottles; the Chardonnay would need a cask, however poor its grain. Strapped across Bihan's back, it creaked with every step into the nearby alley's gloom.

To counter its weakness, Shadi whispered the same cantrip the devil-horned trickster had once toyed with in the sūq. Bihan gagged at the living musk of magic as oily light glittered across the staves. The seams knit and the wood tightened beneath the boy's hands, as if the barrel breathed.

At last, Shadi led them to a tapered, two-storey building, an afterthought wedged between an indoor sūq and a boutique bookseller crowned with polychrome spandrels of fading colour. A neolyt sign sputtered above, blinking in and out of mana like a dying heart—an eyesore in a city of stone and story. But above, the roof told a different tale: greenery spilt from balustrades in lush rebellion. Roses tangled with palms, alchemical vines sagged heavy with berry and bloom.

Shadi's mother, the haunting beauty, had woven her defiance into every leaf and petal. An enchanted garden flaring against the ruin of urban decay.

A cloying sweetness rolled down, cinnamon sharp and far too potent for the city's mana to bear. Magic. No wonder the neolyt stuttered. They followed the scent inside.

Lamps flickered to life in fitful pulses, casting restless shadows that licked the walls and danced across the worn stairwell. The absence of candlelight left the chamber feeling hollow, as if the warmth of flame had been swallowed by the building itself. Rabia shifted beside him, the leather of her gloves creaking, while Shadi gnawed at his nails, the darkened damp of sweat staining his poet's blouse. Bihan heaved the oaken barrel higher on his shoulders, each step up the narrow stairwell a test of balance and patience, the tight corners scraping wood and metal with a metallic groan. At the top, Shadi twisted, whispering to the eyehole of a door. A hollow click answered, and the frame yawned open, then settled back with a groan of reluctant relief.

They slipped inside a library that seemed to inhale the shadows. Towering bookstacks swayed as though on an unseen current, their spines etched with titles that would make Laics blanch and give even seasoned Mystics pause. One volume, however, drew Bihan's gaze like a lodestone: *Aard and the Underground*, by High Mage Montero, Shadi's hallowed teacher. Bihan cradled it, fingers brushing the cracked spine.

The cover shimmered and flickered, conjuring Montero himself, draped in rich blues and burnished golds, tattooed arms bared, one pupil-less eye burning with spectral light, the other missing entirely. Bihan flinched, sensing the gaze of something ancient, familiar yet fleeting, a memory half-remembered, half-buried in the recesses of his skull.

A chill prickled along his spine, conjuring colours of postulant greens and shadowed purples, the drapery of the cruel Vizier of Syrek rising in his mind. Relief rippled through him as he realised the figure was not who he feared. Instead, he allowed himself a small, crooked smile at the image of a self-proclaimed Wizard of Enkhara and High Mage of Aard, Montero, who claimed that magic belonged to nature.

"Put it back," Shadi hissed, tugging a cord. The ceiling groaned as a wooden staircase folded downwards. "She'll know. Mother always knows."

Bihan returned the book, fingertips tingling.

Paintings lined the walls, chronicling magic's rise, its fall, and its clandestine resurgence. Beside Shadi's mother's portrait hung an esoteric parchment, its right corner neatly torn away, leaving only a single name scrawled in its blank space: *Syrek*. Succulents draped every shelf, crowding the floor, their leaves brushing shoes and ankles. At the centre of it all, a blackened chiminea brooded, its soot-darkened surface seeming to harbour secrets of its own. Bihan's eye lingered before following Shadi upwards.

They ascended into a canopy of impossible growth. This was no garden, but a dream made real. Alien flora bristled with buds and fruits that should never endure Enkhara's temperate seasons, yet their scents were proof enough: Thebian wildberries, southern mung beans, and the leathery tang of durian. Pomegranates, plump and jewel-bright, gleamed brighter than any northern sūq stall, though even their sweetness bowed to a ghostly undercurrent of rain in the air, despite no cloud marring the sky.

At the heart of the garden sprawled a vineyard, vines from distant continents twisted together as if drawn from a single, impossibly old rootstock. Shadi—gnat, as Bihan called him—hovered behind, wide-eyed, every branch and tendril a testament to his mother's obsession. Ahead, an ancient staff jutted from a stone railing, split along its length, sapphire light glowing like the sorceress' eyes. Shadi's gasp cut through the murmuring leaves.

"A ward," he warned. "Disturb it, and the garden dies."

Bihan paused, sliding along the terrace beside Rabia, watching Shadi guide them with exacting precision to remove the barrel without brushing the flora. Sweat beaded on the boy's brow as he smoothed back damp, oily hair. "Don't touch that," Shadi said, nodding at the staff. "Good. Follow me."

They edged along the narrow terrace. Shadi slipped between twisted vines like a dancer, each step measured. Bihan's sandal snapped a stray leaf, and Rabia plucked a rogue raspberry, its juice darkening her gloves. At the far edge, Shadi froze, knees trembling. "Here," he whispered. "I won't cross, not while it watches."

Bihan levelled his khopesh, the blade catching the faint glimmer of a fizzling neolyt. "Watches?"

Rabia crouched beneath a grape shoot. "There's nothing here."

Shadi's throat went dry. "You're Laics. Only by stepping in and braving the ward will the illusion break."

"Then lead the way, gnat. Or step aside."

The boy's arms flailed, panic creeping into each word. "It's a terracotta guardian, bound by my mother's spell to protect these grapes. She warned it kills anyone who dares touch them. I won't."

Terror made him almost glow. Bihan gave a curt nod and dipped low, shoulders brushing vine supports. Each careful step churned the damp soil, releasing pearly bubbles that drifted upwards, popping in shrill, bell-like cracks. Rabia followed, the bursts shrieking like tiny, unseen warnings.

From the shadowed rows, the warrior emerged, a hulking terracotta form, tusks curling from its jaw like a stordyr's, a blade taller than a man cradled in its arms. Its unblinking gaze pinned them, silent and merciless.

Rabia edged back. "Those bubbles, what are they?"

Shadi sagged against the wall, voice small. "Another layer of warding against Laics."

Bihan rolled the oaken barrel between bristling clusters, demonstrating a careful twist to free the Syrek grapes. Tiny thistles glinted at each node. Rabia, hands gloved and steady, tore a bunch free in one smooth motion, dark juice oozing over the leather. The terrace brimmed with the scents of crushed leaf, wet earth, and ripe fruit. Bihan drew a long breath, and then a sudden shriek cleaved the air, freezing his blood.

Steel hissed. He ducked as a zweihänder whistled past his head. "Moves stealthily for a heap of stone." He drew his khopesh in one smooth motion, meeting the next swing with a ringing parry. "Rabia, grab the barrel and bolt! Now!"

Rabia snatched two handfuls of grapes, sealed the barrel, and dashed for the stairs, tomahawks clinking at her belt. Shadi stood rooted. Bihan spun low, slashing at the golem's calves. The awkward strike jarred his arm; his grip faltered, khopesh clattering across the mosaic floor. He reached for his dagger, but the golem's soil-scented hand closed around his throat, lifting him, zweihänder poised to cleave.

Pain flared through his chest as he pummelled its forearm. Then—WHACK! A stone struck the golem's temple. Its head jerked, tusked features tightening, and it released him. Both warrior and barbarian turned. Shadi stood trembling, another cobblestone in hand, his violet eyes blazing with fear and something sharper. Defiance. For the briefest instant, Bihan glimpsed more than a cowering gnat. Recognition flickered in the golem's stance, its mute gaze lingering on the boy as though recalling another time. Shadi hurled again, a wild throw that missed, then bolted, heart hammering louder than his feet.

Bihan's chest thumped with pain and something close to pride, though quickly smothered. He rolled away, snatched up his weapons, and cursed. A direct fight was folly.

Then, with a guttural groan, the blackened chiminea burst through the roof, destroying the terrace and upending the staff. A beast of soot and fire, it roared skywards, bearing two figures clinging to its flue.

Shadi's voice carried through the din, coal clutched tight in his hand: "Up here, Bihan! You must jump!"

Bihan scrambled onto the chiminea. Sparks rained as it circled the guardian three times before obeying Shadi's command and taking flight. Below, the last of his mother's vines withered, wards unravelling, rain-clouds congealing as if the sky itself grieved.

They fled east, the first step of Syreki Chardonnay secured at last.

Behind them, the terracotta guardian sank back into silence, resuming its vigil among broken vines and shattered wards. The staff caved inwards with a dull implosion, and clouds massed over the city. Rain began to fall, not born of storm or season, but conjured in mourning, just as Bihan had scented before it ever touched the earth.

VI

The Weight of the Globe

The chiminea spat them onto the far edge of eastern Aledhyn, before a shop Bihan swore had never stood there. Its façade belonged to no craftsmen he knew. Burgundy tiles caught the sun in wavering gleams, a gilt sign proclaiming in ornate strokes *Globes 'R' Us*. The letters shimmered like coins scattered in water. His gaze lingered on the word *globe*, mouth hardening, before he turned to Rabia. She shrugged lightly, telling him the store had last taken root in the southern quarter, back when she dealt with its hobgoblin proprietor.

Bihan's jaw locked. Pocket dimensions were fragile as spun glass, treacherous as quicksand. He'd bristled the first time Rabia even spoke of one. Standing so close to that unseen veil of magic set his skin on edge, yet she pressed forwards with her secret plan, hinting but never revealing.

Shadi, restless, coaxed the chiminea with a fistful of coal to ferry them on towards Seaborne. The vessel hissed in disdain, curled in on itself, and vanished.

"Stunning, isn't it?" Rabia's smile widened at the sight. "If buildings could be beautiful."

The tiles patterned themselves into four-leaf clovers that clung to every wall. A black-tiled gazebo crowned the doorway, its roof propped by slender columns that melted into midnight-blue railings and broad welcoming steps. A sorcerer's tower clung precariously to one flank, as though grafted in desperation by some Mystic eager to prove his name. The air bit sharp with the tang of thaumic resin, acrid and cold on Bihan's tongue. He was tired of magic, of its taste or smell that never quite washed away no matter how you blew your nose or spat.

For a moment he considered abandoning Felipe's folly, letting Camila Callo stumble along her own road. But loose ends gnawed worse than hunger, and his name had been built on never leaving a quest unfinished. If he failed her, regret would stalk him to his grave. He shifted the oaken barrel higher on his shoulders, filled his lungs with the dusty, acrid air, and stepped forwards with Rabia at his flank. Behind them, Shadi fussed with parchment in hand, oil flecking his forehead, nails unbitten, pits no longer stained by sweat. The gnat looked different—composed, almost unrecognisable—and Bihan felt a flicker of reassurance. A calmness in him.

Beyond the white picket fence stretched an oasis at odds with the drab, arid city: hedges clipped neat as soldiers, grass lush and unyielding, as though the ground itself had been transplanted from some kinder land. Bihan reached for the knocker—cast absurdly in the shape of a testicle—when the door groaned open on its own.

A hollow creak ran the length of his spine.

They filed through. Mesquite boards shone under an irregular grid of cabinets; each crammed with antiquities that whispered their long-forgotten histories. At the centre stood a child-sized suit of armour, its gilded helm forged to cradle twin horns. A bronze plaque read: *Torbjörn.* The name nagged at Bihan like a half-remembered song.

Beside it, a glass globe exhaled a soft whistle. Bihan leant close, drawing in the scent of fresh-cut grass. Inside, a tiny man tended his twilight garden until he toppled dead. An instant later the light shifted, the man stood again, sweeping with his broom, whistling anew—only to collapse once more. The loop turned endlessly, serene and horrifying in its inevitability.

"A death-loop," Shadi breathed. "Mother always warned—"

"—that it's impossible?" The voice cut high and sharp, dismissive. Behind a cluttered counter stood a hobgoblin scarcely taller than Rabia. He adjusted a monocle, scratched a pointed ear, and sniffed the air with faint disdain. "Nonsense. Death owed me a favour."

Bihan crossed his arms. "Fregor spoke of such things existing in limericks. Never thought I'd see one. Especially not in a magical shop that doesn't smell the part."

The hobgoblin twitched. "Because I loathe cinnamon." His tongue flicked like a lizard's. "Darragh Donnagan, thaumaturge and globemaker. You're welcome."

Rabia inclined her head. "This is Bihan the Beauty. Shadi. And I'm Rabia, as you know."

"Yes, yes." Darragh rolled his eyes. "I know all the tales about the last Thebian barbarian. All very overstated. And that lump of terracotta clinging to you? I sold its living kin once—truly living—to that boy's mother."

Bihan brushed the residue from his shoulder. "Living terracotta? Imagine that."

"Anyway. What can I do for you? The shop and I are pressed for time. Places to be."

Shadi cocked an eyebrow. "The shop *and* you? Does it stand on a yaga-leg?"

"Yaga-legs are for pretenders," Darragh snapped, a black claw tapping the counter. "I have dignity. You'd be amazed at the marvels a thaumaturge conjures. Would knock the socks off your stinky feet."

Bihan rolled his good eye and lowered the barrel with a thud. "Enough games. Let's talk business, *wonderworker*."

Darragh sprang onto a stool to peer into the barrel. When he caught sight of black-thistle grapes, and Bihan's marble eye throbbing with its low hum, his grin spread slow as oil across his face. He held up a Pocket Globe, empty and expectant. "One moment."

He vanished behind a mahogany staircase that spiralled upwards, its inlays gleaming with a master's pride. Mismatched chandeliers swayed above, promising splendour or escape.

When he returned, it was with a flourish. "I could charge the usual rate... or make an exception."

Bihan's brow rose. "You haven't heard what I want."

"I don't need to." Darragh set the globe on the counter. "You'll enter with the boy."

Bihan's hand brushed his marble eye. "Why's that?"

"Because it's the only way to age Syreki Chardonnay properly," Darragh said, clapping his hands together. "You'd have puzzled it out, given enough time."

The thought of stepping into a pocket dimension curdled Bihan's gut. He hated the way the hobgoblin read him, as if his every need were written on his skin. Foresight or manipulation, he couldn't tell. Still, he pressed three coins of gold into the creature's palm, remembering Rabia's warning: three gold meant three years.

Three coins for three years. And then? Bihan's head gave a slow shake. There had to be another way.

"Relax." Darragh's grin quivered in the lamplight, a flame playing at the edge of smoke. "I'll set the globe for twelve years—exactly twelve. Enough to ripen the wine to your captain's craving. After that, you'll find Camila Callo. With her... ah, best not to ruin the tale."

Shadi leant over the counter, pupils wide as coins. "But you must! How do you—"

Bihan's glare snapped him shut. "He mustn't. I'll not carry more of the future than I must. One answer only: if I agree, will Camila see home again?"

The hobgoblin tilted a shoulder. A shrug. No more.

A rough breath clawed its way free of Bihan. "Then name your price."

Darragh's monocle winked. "A story. From your boyhood to the slaughter of your people. No one has chronicled the Thebian way—a barbarian's way. Not really. You can."

Heat seared beneath Bihan's skin, old scars splitting open. Hearth-fires, drill yards, the sting of iron against his knuckles—then ash, smoke, screams. Syrek, too. He'd buried these memories beneath silence, yet the hobgoblin's words pressed a lever against that barricade.

Bihan pried the barrel open and pressed thumb to grape. His skin broke with a muffled sigh, bleeding red that curled down his hand like a worm writhing from soil. The sight steadied him. He caught the key at his neck, gripped it until the edge cut his palm. Blood welled, trickling to merge with his thumb's rivulet. The wider the pool, the wider the barricade inside him became until the flood of memory came through.

A blaze caught in his eye. He nodded once.

Darragh broke into a jig, his feet (in thin, smelly slippers) clicking like dice on wood. From beneath the counter, he drew a dozen globes. Each rested on a sand-dusted base of broken swords and half-crushed skulls, streaked in dried crimson that might once have been more than paint.

"Neat, eh?" He ran a black nail across a skull's curve. "I thought to fictionalise your tale for my shelves. Though these days the erotic globes fetch faster coin. Bookshops and wholesalers glut on them like pigeons on grain."

"My mother said fiction breeds grief," Shadi murmured.

"Suicides, mostly." Darragh flapped a hand. "But I deal in happiness, so I sleep untroubled." He tapped the largest globe, its skin of glass trembling. "The prototype. Copies follow, tweaked for historians, lovers of the macabre, and collectors with rare appetites."

Bihan's leg began to tremble, not from fear but from strain. Memories pressed, unbidden: dawn drills with his father, his mother's soft laughter, the sept's iron codes. He locked eyes with the hobgoblin, certain the true cost ran deeper than words.

He shut the barrel with a hard thud. "Let's begin."

The words spilt a river. His telling ran clean, strong as snowmelt cutting a gorge. Shadi's attention was given to his parchment, but his gaze kept snaring on Bihan's marble eye, drawn to its dark hum.

Darragh coaxed a cloud of shadow into the globe. "Structure. Hierarchies. Kilts. Leave nothing vague."

"Alihan Hammerfist," Bihan began. "My father. Last and greatest Khan of the Thebian Khanate."

He spoke of victories and the drills at dawn, the sting of the morning's bite in his lungs, his mother's stern grace and lessons in etiquette. Her smile glimmered before him, but her hair slipped away in the haze of memory—brown? fair? He stumbled, swallowed ache, pressed on.

When Bihan spoke of Alihan's challenges, he told of them not as contests but as reckonings. Every warrior who challenged his rule was mercilessly struck down, yet their deaths were remembered not as defeats but as honours—final benedictions granted by the khan's own hand. To fall beneath Alihan's blade was to be immortalised, one's family exalted in the echo of his triumphs. His hand closed around his father's broken sword, and he smiled, memory at last unclouded.

"A khan could never lay down his mantle; he could only fall in combat or be unseated in challenge," he said. "The title was never given but seized—born in blood, trial, or conquest. If a khan died in his bed, he'd be dishonoured."

Be that as it may, Bihan saw himself gone to grey, his body shrunken and bent as a dried reed, breath ebbing in a bed of linen rather than dust. The thought was a heresy stitched deep in his marrow, for a khan was meant to blaze out beneath steel or fire, not fade like dusk across a field. Yet the vision lingered, treacherous and sweet: the weight of age in his bones, the slow unravelling of years, a death measured not by conquest but by time's patient hand.

Darragh's knuckled fingers drifted over the globe's surface, coaxing shadows and light into shape as if shaping the world itself. "And that goes for all barbarians?" he asked, voice tight with curiosity.

"Yes." Bihan flexed his fingers against the sticky warmth of blood still clinging to his palm. "Every khanate traces its rites back to Thebes."

He spoke on, the words a river of memory, until even the thaumaturge's practiced hands faltered, hesitating when the narrative darkened with the slaughter of Bihan's people.

"Summarise," Darragh rasped, voice brittle. "Please."

Bihan closed his good eye, letting the black marble hum against his brow, and summoned the vision. Flames devoured fields as he hid in his uncle's cellar. Huts shuddered and collapsed. The longhouse imploded. His father strode at the vanguard, mother at his side, pressing his grandfather's khopesh into Alihan's grasp. Ash drifted like snow in the thick, coppery scent of blood and magic, clinging to skin and hair, tangling with the heat that'd singed hearth and home.

Rabia brushed his hand. He wrenched away. "Two orbs in the smoke—eyes aflame with sorcery. The sickly-sweet odour of magic. Cinnamon. The glowing-eyed demon snapped his fingers. Alihan's sword shattered. My father fell." Bihan dryly gulped. "My mother's cry... strangled."

Bihan's head sagged forwards.

Ash from his past coated his throat. The cellar's walls pressed against his cheek as he cried. Beams aflame cracked above. Silence fell where mother's voice should've been. The city of Syrek emerged instead. His father's face smudged. His mother's hair, lost to time. The good dissolved, leaving ruin's taste. And Bihan forced the tide of memories back down; the struggle etched into every tendon of his hand.

Shadi broke the hush. "You're a khan, then. The last to walk Enkhara's earth."

Bihan's jaw tightened. "No. I'm not. I forfeited that title with my cowardice." His good eye fixed on the hobgoblin. "So, we use the alpha globe?"

Darragh sniffed. "You've given me enough to script thirteen years, four months, and seven days of your boyhood in Thebes. So, no. You'll use a replica. Twelve years. Clean, exact. No filler. I only work in years."

He snapped his clawed fingers. Shelves trembled as empty globes swelled with black vapour, roiling like storm clouds sealed in glass. He offered tea while the magic brewed. Rabia accepted, drifting towards the sun-scorched and battered armour, whispering the name etched into its plaque. Shadi waved the cup away, eyes tethered to his parchment. Bihan drummed the barrel lid, his impatience ringing in the quiet like a knuckle on a tombstone.

"Wait—damn it! We're missing something." He leant forwards, growling. "We've grapes, but they're uncrushed."

Rabia sipped without looking up. "Have a barbarian do it inside the globe."

Darragh's finger shot skywards. "No. The ageing begins the instant the barrel enters. And if you want Syreki Chardonnay, not some gutter plonk fit for copper-purses, the grapes must be crushed by a hand—or foot—that knows the craft."

Shadi glanced up, brow furrowed. "Couldn't we go in, recruit an expert, then begin ageing at the right time? Or here's a thought—make the globe last twelve years and one month. Problem solved."

Darragh's nostrils flared, his nail stabbing the air. "Whole years only. That's the law of it. If you'd listened instead of pawing at that ridiculous spell, you'd know." Shadi bristled, but Darragh cut him down with a glare. "And don't make me spell out why thirteen won't do when you need twelve. You're not a fool. At least, I hope you're not."

Bihan caught on the word *spell*. So that's what Shadi guarded so tightly. A spell for what? His mind darted to the torn sheet framed in his mystical home, the single name at its heart. Suspicion coiled, a slow tightening in his gut.

He leant back, feigning ease with a lazy shrug. "If we fail, we try again." His fingers brushed the rim of his artificial eye, its low hum passing into his skin. "You've more than one of these globes."

Darragh's shoulders stiffened. "Too many variables!" His words cracked with impatience. "I won't waste my craft on what-ifs. I'll bend time for you, coin and schedule, but my globes are sacrosanct. And where, pray tell, will you pluck more of those precious grapes, thickhead?"

A vein hammered in his temple, his jaw clenched until Bihan half-expected it to splinter.

With a snap of his heels, the hobgoblin broke from the quarrel. "Fresh tea," he announced, disdain curling his lips. He slipped off one slipper, then the other, and vanished into the back. His steps echoed through the boards, clipped and precise.

Moments later he reappeared, cradling a wide, shallow bowl and a wooden stool. He set them on the counter with priestly deliberation. "I wasn't always a thaumaturge," he said. His trouser legs rolled to the knee with a flourish, revealing wiry calves dusted in auburn hair. He cast Bihan a sidelong glance, eyebrow cocked in mockery. "Best take a moment, while I prepare the grapes."

VII

Twelve Years, a Memory

Night pressed close about Darragh's shop, candle flames shivering across floorboards sticky with half-drunk tea and scattered cups. The hobgoblin's bare feet whispered through crushed Syreki grapes, each step releasing a prickly perfume that drifted into the rafters and lingered like incense. Rabia knelt before Torbjörn's battered armour, fingertips grazing the gilded plaque as though the steel itself might grant counsel. Shadi bent low over his parchment, lips shaping muted syllables, ears tilted to catch every cadence of Bihan's tale.

Bihan leant against a raftered beam, timbre low and steady, as he spoke of the basalt stelae hidden in the western pyramids—his payment for the hobgoblin's winemaking. At their mention, he saw Darragh's shoulders stiffen, the hobgoblin's knuckles whitening against the oaken barrel's rim. Silence gathered, broken only by the slow drip of amber juice from Darragh's toes, coalescing where the grapes' sharp skins had left fine rivulets of blood.

"Easy," Bihan murmured, stepping forwards. He leant over, sweeping fingers through the mingled pool, and looked up with a steadying glance. "Are you hurt?"

Darragh raised his head, brow furrowed so deep his leathery skin seemed chiselled by age. With a decisive click he adjusted his monocle, candlelight flaring across its lens. His whisper unfurled, a hiss slicing the stillness like cracked glass.

"Wyverns. That's what Toussaint hunts."

The word dropped between them, heavy with ancient fury and the bitter promise of vengeance from the throneless.

Shadi jerked upright, parchment slipping from his fingers as the flamelight leapt across his startled eyes. "Wyverns?" His disbelief rattled the syllables. "But... if they endure, it's only in legend. If exposed, their lungs would shrivel, their scales would crumble at fever's touch. How can such vulnerable beasts—infants of the world—stir an uprising? How does their myth breathe life into Al-Qiyamah?"

The hush returned, broken only by the hiss of burning wicks. Even Rabia's fingers stilled on the plaque, as though time itself held its breath. The weight of Toussaint's design—taming the fierce, the almost-forgotten—hung in the room, daring belief.

With a shove, Darragh sent the barrel skidding across the counter. It struck a tower of tea caddies, porcelain shattering in a spray of shards. He ignored the ruin; eyes fixed instead on Rabia's reverent gaze. Then he dipped a finger into the barrel, lifted a bead of amber liquid on his blackened nail, and tasted. A subtle nod confirmed his satisfaction. He drew a soft cloth from his pocket, wiping feet and shins clean of grape-stain.

"Forget the western stelae," he growled. "The one you seek lies in Seaborne. A stele inscribed to guide its bearer to this whispered race—dragon-kin, the same Freja Torbjörn died protecting. With them, Toussaint will challenge the great sapphire dragon of the south, clear a path to his throne, and reclaim it unopposed. Dragon-kin at his flank will make him unstoppable. A legend fit for Al-Qiyamah."

The name struck Bihan like an iron in the chest: Freja Torbjörn. His thoughts stuttered before meaning could settle. The khorvo general who'd once led him and Rabia into the Syrek War against the Vizier, only to vanish in their darkest hour and abandon the city to ruin. All threads knotted here. Rabia—childhood devotee of her kin—knelt now before sun-bleached armour, torn between veneration and betrayal.

And Camila Callo: her march west with Toussaint's loyalists, the rumours of scattered stelae, the sudden redirection to Seaborne... Bihan saw the shape of her aim as clearly as a map. His hand tightened around the key at his throat. Camila and her trail mattered above all. He would find her. He must.

"Let's enter the globe," he said. "Now."

Darragh slipped back into his slippers, curt in tone. "Rules first. You must will yourselves in. If you falter, another may will you—with consent. Inside, twelve years pass. Here, only twelve minutes. Take heart: you'll not wear the skin of the globe's protagonist, a child Bihan, but yourselves. Unless you wish for bespoke avatars. No? Very well."

"Twelve years?" Bihan groaned. "You jest."

"Oh, he does not." Rabia rose from her kneel, her words keener than steel.

"Then so be it." Bihan turned to Shadi with a rare smile. "Twelve years on the road with me, and you'll lack for little. Might even make a decent ward of you yet." He extended a hand. "Hobgoblin, the map of eastern Enkhara."

After a pause, Darragh slid the crinkled parchment across. Bihan unfurled it, weighing the corners with a pocket watch, a teacup, a moonstone, and a mechanical bird. He tapped a mark northwest of Thebes.

"My uncle's abandoned cellar—the one I told of. Once inside, leave the barrel there, Shadi. Swiftly, and unseen."

He lifted the key from around his neck, its metal catching firelight, and dangled it before the Mystic.

"Your key? You've kept it all this time as a reminder of—"

"My failure." Bihan pressed it into Shadi's palm. "I can't face that cellar again. That is your burden. *Do not* let another witness you. My uncle's key still exists in their world; it'll draw their curiosity. The wine must rest in silence."

Darragh's nail rapped the counter. "Correct. What you carry in, may come out. But what lies within already—regrets, secrets—must remain."

Bihan caught Shadi's chin, forcing his gaze to meet his own. "No one unsealed that cellar until my people fell. Keep it so. Don't give them cause to pry." He straightened, softening with a smile. "I'll wait on the outskirts with two horses."

"Not camels?" Shadi tucked the key into his vest, eyes brightening with mischief. "Don't worry, Bihan. I'll manage."

Night deepened as Darragh guided their fingers across the globe. Thebes rose in splendour beneath them, and Bihan's chest swelled with a joy he hadn't felt in years. He breathed in the imagined scent of linseed oil—sun-warmed, resinous—his grandfather's tradition, coating every blade of the khanate.

A rent in drifting cloud revealed the longhouse at the settlement's heart, thorn-thatch gleaming against its redwood beams. And there lay the cellar. Bihan's throat closed at the sight, the dread of youth crawling back into him.

A trainer's bark rang sharp through the air, followed by the thunk of arrows sinking into cork. His father's stern intonations drew him back to those merciless drills: blade against tin soldiers, exercises in contempt for armour. Alihan had taught that to bare one's chest was to live unshackled.

Weightless, Bihan drifted down through the cloud-break. Thebes widened, swelling towards him.

He touched earth beside the stables, and Shadi landed moments later, Bihan's key clutched tight. While the boy headed for the cellar, Bihan offered two imaginary gold coins for destriers. The stablemaster refused. Those belonged to the Khan and his wife. So, when his back turned, Bihan stole the beasts, riding them out with haste, wary of neighbours' eyes.

He kept his gaze low as he signalled Shadi to the waiting mounts. In one fluid motion, the boy slid the barrel into the cellar's dark mouth and emerged unseen. Bihan's pulse thundered. This world was perilously real. He understood, then, why some of Darragh's patrons never came back whole—why they staggered from the globe haunted by lives suspended mid-breath. The wonderworker's craft was almost flawless. Almost.

They mounted and rode east beneath a sun that neither set nor rose yet moved with its own solemn rhythm. Bihan swore not to squander a moment of the twelve years gifted within this prism of time. Together they charted the length of Enkhara, crossed into neighbouring lands, even boarded a westbound ship, only to be chased from Seaborne's bay by pyrates before setting foot on shore.

In time, Shadi pleaded for arcane tutelage. Bihan, gnawed by superstition, yielded at last. Better the Mystic he knew than the one he didn't. And here, before the Great Purge, magic thrived in the open. At first, they sought vagrant sorcerers but eventually placed themselves under Basem Alpheniq of Spellforge: a true magus, if ever one could be.

Years folded. Under Alpheniq's guardianship, Shadi's thirst for forbidden lore led him dangerously close to a necromantic incantation that might've cast him out. Only a humbled apology secured his place. Four years passed in the vaulted mountain halls, the boy emerging with a patchy beard, hair in untamed knots.

By the sixth year, Bihan had grown accustomed even to the reek of spellcraft. They returned to Enkhara. Shadi married a hashishiyah shah's daughter, divorced her for a camel within a week, and escaped her father's enraged elephant by a whisker—thanks only to Bihan's knowledge of hashishiyah lore.

By the seventh year, Syrek's gothic gates rose before them. Bihan's teeth chattered at the gargoyled arches, his gut heaving with memories of a war he knew this false realm would never relive. He forced himself to breathe. This wasn't real. Yet the city towered too vividly to dismiss.

Tenfold the size of Aledhyn, Syrek loomed like a fortress of shadow. Its obsidian brickwork absorbed the lantern glow, every wall cut with uncanny precision. Stained glass pulsed sickly green, as though the city itself watched intruders with baleful eyes. Below the Vizier's spire, the streets rose in a rigid grid, roofs bristling with iron rods to summon lightning—a khorvo craft older than mana itself, the very invention that'd once bound Freja Torbjörn to the Vizier.

At the spire's foot, Shadi unrolled the parchment he'd carried through every year. Bihan watched his lips move in reverence, his eyes widening with comprehension... at last. Doubt ebbed from Bihan's chest. There was more to the gnat's heritage than frail hands and fevered study. Something wound deep, tied to his mother, to that framed parchment scrawled with Syrek's name in their home. The captain's half-forgotten warning, however, ghosted through Bihan's mind: someone in

Aledhyn sought to resurrect the city, but he dismissed it. He trusted Shadi now, more than a drunkard's idle gossip.

In Syrek, Shadi fashioned a quarterstaff from cedar so finely balanced it might've come from Spellforge itself, the next step on his path as a magus, just as Basem had instructed. Pride lit the boy brighter than any mana-lamp, though he knew he could never bring it back to the waking world. One day, he would be forced to return to the pearwood wand.

But Bihan hadn't brought them to Syrek for staff or study. He'd come to confront the Vizier spoken of only in hushed, fearful whispers; to look into the eyes of the man fated to bring such ruin and know why.

They found him cloaked in heavy robes; head bowed beneath his hood. Bihan's heart thundered. With a roar he lunged, only to be stopped cold by a force that locked his ankles. He crashed to the cobbles, grit stinging his tongue, dread surging through his chest. When he lifted his gaze, he met the squat and broad shadow of General Freja Torbjörn. Her plate was scarred, her horns lifting like ancient sentinels above the battlefield. Bihan stammered an apology, the marble eye intensely shivering. She gave no answer, only jabbed a stubby finger towards Shadi, a guttural growl warning them to leave.

Yet they did not. For years they remained, poring through Syrek's archives, burying themselves in dust-heavy tomes and brittle scrolls, hunting whispers of basalt stelae, wyverns, and that fleeting, uneasy bond between Freja and the Vizier. In the final days, one truth burnt through the haze of conjecture: the Seaborne stele was not Megaran-forged. Its maker remained veiled, but its inscription—Megaran or no—hinted at the key to the hidden race.

They had to return to Thebes.

By the skin of their teeth, they reached the settlement and clawed at a dune that'd swallowed the cellar whole. Shadi scraped diligently at the sand-choked mouth, but time slipped away, so Bihan shouldered him aside, tearing the drift free with his own hands. Key clutched tight, his heart pounded as he wrenched open the door and crossed the threshold for the first time in years.

The past erupted. Fear coiled in his chest like a living thing. He saw his mother's hair blazing red. Not blonde, not brown, but a fiery hue brighter than any torch. He felt again the presence of his father: broad yet lithe and swift, the man whose temper had carved Bihan's own resolve.

Memory crashed over him in relentless waves, pulling him down into that dreaded cellar.

Dumbstruck, he dropped to his knees, tracing the gouge where his boyhood self had cowered, watching his parents fall beneath the glowing-eyed Mystic. The crime that'd hardened him against their kind. Yet when his gaze met Shadi's steady, unflinching eyes, the old hatred faltered. The sickly-sweet tang of magic, once enough to wrench his stomach, now pleasantly mingled with the scents of scorched timber and falling rain.

One sour grape needn't spoil the bushel.

Older now in mind, Bihan rose with the barrel hoisted to his shoulder. The key glinted cold between thumb and fore-finger, a tether to a past no longer needed. He smiled and let it fall. It struck the dust with a dull chime; its secrets emptied at last. A soft voice called his name. He looked up. A torchlit figure stood in the doorway: a scraggy-haired boy, his younger self, curious and unafraid.

The sight hollowed his chest. It was time. He drew a breath... and the world shifted.

The key's echo rang on, softening into the faint clink of glass. Smoke and rain curled into beeswax and cork, and the boy with the torch lingered for a heartbeat longer before thinning into candlelight. Shadows stretched into rows of an-tiquities; shelves rose around him like old trees. Darragh pol-ished his monocle in the hush of the shop, and on the counter sat the Syreki Chardonnay, its bouquet twelve years richer.

VIII

The Unquiet Eye

Bihan blinked. The familiar musk of varnished wood and old tomes tugged him back from the distant echoes of Thebes still clinging to his mind. Candlelight shimmered across rows of shelves; the muted slur of tea-drinkers and the low hum of gossip replaced the clang and smoke of his homeland. He lifted his hands, marvelling at calloused palms now freed from twelve years of phantom labour. The age spots were gone, though his soul felt carved by centuries. A pang stirred in his chest—yearning for acrid smoke, for rain-wet timber, for the cinnamon wind of Spellforge and its surroundings. Then came joy.

Memories once sealed behind grief bloomed in brilliant hues, spilling warmth into his chest. He drew a long breath of the shop's air and let a smile crease his lips.

"Welcome back!" Darragh's booming accent crashed through the haze. "Twelve years for you; twelve minutes for us. Although, given the company, it felt like an age to me. Oh! You'll want to read what's beneath that globe."

Bihan leant over Shadi's shoulder. The boy, adjusting once more to his young form, tilted the pocket-world to reveal a plaque fixed in brass:

POCKET GLOBE

Created by Darragh Donnagan (~~Second Period, Amity Era~~ / First Period, Industrial Era)
NOTE: Dispense of your purchase within seconds of returning. Preferably across the room or outside. Your choice.

Cold panic clawed at Bihan. He tore the sphere from Shadi's grip and staggered right, then left, before flinging it skywards. The globe struck a chandelier and burst like thunder. Dragons of glass and light unfurled in a riot of colour, wings scattering rainbows before collapsing into sparks. Crystal shards showered the quartet.

Darragh tsked. "The note didn't specify destroying my chandeliers as an option. Lucky for you, they're easily mended. For me, at least."

Bihan's hand brushed the oaken barrel of Syreki Chardonnay. He feared its taste would sour his tongue with memories of Syrek, yet he bowed his thanks as the shop began its subtle hop through space.

Soon after, they stood on Aledhyn's docks. The captain raised the Chardonnay to his lips, sipped once, and with a pleased grunt granted them passage on the *Delphine*. Their horses were led below deck, their reins already claimed by the crew, but Bihan cared nothing for loss. Each step carried him nearer to Camila Callo Contreras.

On deck, the captain pressed them for tales of Syrek. His eyes gleamed at mention of its black spires and the Vizier's shadow. Bihan and Shadi spoke cautiously, yet when they described the khorvo general standing guard at the Vizier's side, the captain scoffed. His reports, he said, showed no such need of protection. Especially by *that* khorvo.

Bihan's fingertips and toes tingled.

The *Delphine* cut across the Shamrock Sea, its hull splitting green waves that shimmered like emerald glass. At meals they drank only with fish, the Syreki Chardonnay pouring pale gold into tin cups. Afterwards, Bihan would lean against the rail and surrender his gaze to the horizon. No mana-bleached sky. No throngs or chains of duty to an exaggerated legend. Only the boundless sea. It felt divine in its purity—though no all-knowing, all-seeing figurehead shaped such grandeur, only the lawless hand of nature.

The Khanate had never bent to divinities. Strength was creed enough. The priests and peddlers of holy mysteries were charlatans, and Bihan had dismissed them all. Even Rabia's Great Smith could not sway him. Why pray to a hammer when one could forge one's own fate?

Still, when his gaze strayed to Shadi, he wondered. Was the boy pious? Did his parchment spell sing as a prayer, or whisper something darker? Bihan couldn't shake the memory of Shadi's mirth in Syrek, lips curling at forbidden words. His fingertips and toes tingled faintly, yet when no further intensity stirred, he forced his doubts to silence.

That night, however, unease gnawed him.

Off the coast of their destination, a nightmare seized him: Thebes burnt. Roofbeams collapsed into pyres, and the cries of his childhood friends split the hellfire. He wore purple-and-green robes, a quarterstaff alive with crackling sorcery. When a barbarian lunged, he answered with a cantrip, clean and merciless, the man falling in a spray of embers. Yet Bihan couldn't look away. The scene unfurled as if his own body were its puppeteer, every motion shackled to some unseen hand.

A flare of light revealed a red-haired woman struggling beneath his grip. His nails—painted a grotesque fuchsia—bit into the olive skin of her throat until her breath guttered out. When the corpse hit the mud, her face rolled towards him. His mother's face. His knees failed. He reached, but the vision pressed on. His father snatched up his splintered sword, only for acid rain to fall in sheets, stripping flesh from bone, dripping muscle into the blood already pooling at his feet.

The body Bihan wore laughed.

Then the sky tore open. Magenta lightning lanced Syrek's spires as war seethed through the streets and surrounding fields. A pain like molten iron burnt through his left eye. Light burst—blinding, white-hot. And then it ceased. He looked down. In his palm lay a white marble, tattooed skin glowing around it. A black dot bloomed across its surface, spreading like rot, swallowing the purity whole.

Bihan jolted awake, drenched in a salt sheen, ripping the clammy sheets from his bare flesh. His heart thundered as if beating against iron bars, and a tremor he couldn't master seized every limb. The ship's gentle sway brought no solace; Rabia's thunderous snores only worsened the disarray. Beside him, Shadi lay stiff as a spear, eyes glinting from the shadows, fixed on him with unnerving patience.

Bihan pressed a trembling hand to his false eye. The memory of that pristine white marble resting in the tattooed palm. The orb's ceaseless hum rattled inside his head; its rhythm sharpened until blood welled along the scarred rims of eyelid and cheek. Since the voyage began, its vibrations had increased tenfold—whether stirred by the boundless sea or the ship's tight confines, he couldn't say.

Panic tore him from the bunk. He staggered up the stairwell, burst onto the deck, and collapsed to his knees as the night's breath gnawed his skin. The frigid wind drove him to the bowsprit, where he curled against the timber, teeth chattering. And there they came. Three figures flickered into being, mist for flesh yet clear in shape: a rotund man with a flowing beard to the left; a gaunt, bejewelled wraith to the right; and between them, a broad-hipped woman with a heavy braid falling over her shoulder. She reached for him. Drawn by a force he couldn't resist, Bihan reached back.

As her face came into focus, grief hollowed her features. The barrel merchant from Aledhyn. She spoke no word, only wept, her hand passing through his like fog. He longed for warmth, for the solid weight of another, but her fingers stayed insubstantial. Then her touch chilled to ice, etching a searing circle in his palm before she and the others dissolved. The ache remained, phantom and cruel, and Bihan stumbled backwards.

Clutching the railing, he vomited into the black waters. His eye throbbed; in madness he near-tore it free. A rogue wave slammed the bowsprit, drenching his naked frame in spray so biting it snapped him back into himself. The shock of sea-cold steadied him; his breath slowed, his pulse eased. He stared into the ink-black ocean, transformed by the night, the marble remaining a part of his body and soul.

The marble was white, not black, he told himself. *They're not the same.*

"All right?" Shadi's voice came from behind, warmer than the night. "I've only seen you like that once before."

Bihan didn't turn. "Syrek. Damnable place."

Shadi settled at his side, weight solid against the shifting deck. "You know you can talk to me, mate."

Bihan's thoughts flickered to the parchment hidden in Shadi's vest. Their bond had been tempered through years of hardship; he wouldn't risk it over dreams, however vivid. Perhaps the marble was the same, perhaps not. Best to leave the truth untouched while trust still held thread thin. So instead, they spoke of the Pocket Globe's wonders, weaving stories until dawn bled pale across the horizon and the crew stirred.

"You've grown into a good man," Bihan said at last, rare tenderness in his tone.

Shadi smirked faintly. "Not a gnat any longer?"

"You'll always be a gnat." Bihan cuffed his arm, gentler than the words. "But you're my gnat. Now, where's my kilt before I give the crew a fright?"

By afternoon, the captain summoned them to his quarters with promises of food and wine. Rabia bristled, unwelcoming of the captain's deformed face; her glare smouldering as she watched him carve through fish flesh and potatoes. Bihan, unbothered, took the offer gladly. The man's scarred face mirrored his own; there was comfort in that kinship of wounds, the same odd solace he'd felt with the barrel merchant.

They sat at a low table burdened with fruit and Syreki Chardonnay. The captain's belly shook as he offered a bowl of dates. "What made you leave your hashishiyah wife? Their beauty's said to be unequal."

Shadi leant back, one brow arched. "She was legendary. As graceful as an oasis among sand and wyrm, but too relentless for a Mystic's constitution."

Bihan sipped the Chardonnay. Its amber warmth carried a faint tang of iron—the blood of Darragh, infused with the wine twelve long years.

Rabia snorted. "He fled, captain." Her laugh cut through the lantern's haze. "Before her father could trample him with an elephant."

The captain dabbed at his cheek scar. "And how'd you manage that?"

Bihan stretched, poured another cup, and plucked a pomegranate from the bowl. "We rode four days across the dunes to the cliffs of Enkhara. Then leapt into the rogue seas below. Hashishiyah won't follow there."

Their laughter swelled until a shout from above signalled anchor-drop. The captain's gaze strayed to the wine, envy threading with admiration. "I never asked why you sail to Seaborne. It's a land of chains and misery, where the only thing on the itinerary is forced labour."

Bihan split the pomegranate; its tangy-sweet perfume filled the cabin. "We seek a woman named Camila Callo Contreras," he said, tossing arils into his mouth. "She left Aledhyn for Seaborne."

The captain's smile was brittle, like glass stretched too thin. "Is she beautiful?"

"Stunning," Shadi replied, plain and unflinching. "My mother showed her face in an oasis pool. Simple magic. Foolproof."

"Golden skin, dirty-blonde hair, eyes so deep you'd drown in them—hazel with a streak of blue at one corner, henna tracing her slender fingers and pretty feet," Bihan said, voice low as a tide. "She's embraced Aledhyn as home. Its culture now her own."

The captain's smile stretched unnaturally. His cheeks creased, and a droplet of saliva trickled from his scar onto his chest. Whether it was the wine or something older stirring beneath it, Bihan could've sworn a flicker of something familiar danced behind the captain's right eye. A glow faint but insistent, like a memory clawing its way back into the room.

Unnerved, his fingertips tingled, and he rose.

"We'll disembark at first light," Bihan said, tossing the pomegranate aside and polishing his chalice. "We're paid in full, captain. Thank you for sharing the Chardonnay."

The two men clasped forearms in a firm, echoing grip. "May our paths cross again soon, barbarian," the captain rumbled, the glow flickering once more.

Dawn broke with a hush over Seaborne's cove. The *Delphine* settled gently, and Bihan's breath caught at the view. Black basalt cliffs at the water's edge softened into ribbons of ash-grey and chalk-white, then erupted into the richest emerald of pine-clad peaks. Waterfalls traced silver scars down the mountainsides, spilling mist into the turquoise bay. Below, the beach gleamed pure as milk, its gentle surf kissing swaying palms, half-submerged kegs rotting in the sand, a lone skeleton clutching a rusty cutlass, and a single, sea-worn bottle nestled among seashells.

This wasn't the ragtag settlement he'd known in the Pocket Globe. Here, the Corsair King's lust for grandeur had banished squalor. Pyrates had become corsairs; their hovels replaced by coral-white facades that gleamed in the sun. Bihan drew a long, bracing breath of salt-tinged air. Familiar, yet altogether changed.

He turned to Shadi and Rabia. "We swim under cover of the eastern headland, slip past that palm grove, then follow the caravan of slavedrivers," he traced the route in the air with a finger, eye scanning the cliffs and surf. "Look like we belong. No funny business."

Rabia's jaw was a knot of muscle, eyes burning as she spat a curse into the churning sea. "A khorvo can't swim," she snarled, "but I'll be damned if I sink on my own watch." Her knuckles went bone-white on the tomahawks' hafts, every muscle in her arms coiled tight as a spring.

Shadi slid the folded parchment into his vest, securing the pearwood wand along his sleeve, and gave a sharp nod.

Bihan's stomach knotted with anticipation, hunger, and nerves. "On my mark: Rabia first."

She teetered at the rail, curses blooming like dark flowers on her lips, until Bihan caught her shoulders and hurled her into the gentle surf. Her scream cleaved the dawn air, fizzing into a torrent of Megaran invective as she bobbed upright, hair plastered with salt and sunlight glinting off her tall and proud horns.

Shadi followed, a shadow slipping into the depths with the grace of a stalking predator.

Bihan drew a lungful of briny air, bracing himself, then sprang into the surf. Cold struck his chest and lungs, rolling beneath him in eager, churning waves. Foam kissed his cheeks, salt licked his hair, and the pull of the current tugged at his limbs, coaxing him forwards. Yet beneath the sting and drag, a savage clarity bloomed: the untamed promise of what lay ahead, sharp and intoxicating as the first strike of a blade.

IX

Where Ambition Dies

The wavelets of Seaborne's wide cove bore them inwards like an embrace, carrying with them the distant cries of auctioneers. The voices ricocheted off the black cliffs, harsh counterpoint to the gentle hush of water lapping against their limbs. The bay gleamed a lucid blue, clearer even than the central oases of Enkhara. Tadpoles darted, silver fish gathered in hopeful shoals, and on the banks, curious faces watched as Bihan and Shadi swam while Rabia clung white-knuckled between them.

Black-skinned natives lounged on the sand, pipes trailing smoke in slow spirals. Mixed-race sailors unloaded heavy crates bound for the auction, each chest a promise of profit. Beside them shuffled men, women, and children in chains, herded by swollen overseers with whips coiled at their belts. It was a perverse pageant: luxury and cruelty marched hand in hand.

The place had changed. What'd once been a ragged pyrate cove now gleamed with pretence. The beach lay smoothed and combed, as though crafted by artisans rather than the tide. Corsairs had shed their tattered sails for tricorn hats and brocade coats, but behind the polish their trade had not altered. They still trafficked in flesh, still killed with cheerful ease, only now beneath a veneer of civility.

Emerging at the eastern headland, they wrung the brine from their hair and passed beneath a stand of palms. Bihan's gaze climbed to Seaborne's most fearsome landmark: the colossal ship perched high on the central mountain; its timbers fused with rock as though grown there. Sails billowed, though no wind could claim them, and its vast shadow brooded over the city. He wondered if the ancient stele lay hidden amid the old rigging and centuries of loot.

Had Camila Callo been hauled into that silent leviathan? A knot cinched tight in his chest. The fortress-ship was no relic. It was the city's heart, a grim monument to plunder raised into permanence. The docks below, however, sang no shanties. No painted courtesans leant from balconies. Instead, a dark-skinned overseer guided his chain-gang with a mere glance, cruelty distilled to ritual. Seaborne had burnished its surface, but the stain beneath remained.

Falling into step with the line of captives, the three wound their way towards the city's heart. The slums gave way to cobblestones cut broad as a parade ground. Foundations mimicked the cyclopean blocks of Megaran ruins, while above them straight-lined houses and tea-houses rose in eastern symmetry. Mana-lamps burnt pale at every corner, casting the streets in a counterfeit daylight.

Corsair nobles strode those avenues with cutlasses at their hips and tricorns cocked in careful indifference. They bowed with clipped courtesy, smiled with painted restraint, and spoke through masks crafted as artfully as any porcelain façade.

At last, the road spilt into the bazaar, and they entered the auction's source. The market sprawled broader than any sūq of Aledhyn, arranged in great concentric rings. At its centre, human lives were paraded in pairs, chained and catalogued like livestock. Families ripped apart, children bartered as investments. From gilt balconies above, patrons in velvet and silk surveyed the stock with cold appraisal, weighing not faces but prices.

Bihan turned his attention aside, memory pricking with the sight of half-starved parents gnawing boiled leather to keep from death. He guided Rabia and Shadi to the bazaar's quieter fringe, where stalls overflowed with marvels: extinct pelts soft as whisper, Ophiri sandalwood burning in brass bowls, gems from khorvo mines glowing with inner fire, Aledhyn glass shimmering beside fine eastern porcelain.

Yet what caught him was a pomegranate. He tested its skin, listening for the perfect give beneath his thumb. One answered his scrutiny. He set it down again without coin, hand resting casually on the curve of his khopesh.

"Camila Callo Contreras," he said, raising a heavy brow. "Where?"

The portly merchant pressed a calloused finger to his lips, tossed the fruit back at him, then jabbed a hand towards the mountain-ship. In that spare gesture, Bihan heard all he needed. Rabia muttered sharp denial, Shadi echoed her disbelief, but the merchant ignored them and barked for a corsair guard.

Bihan inclined his head in thanks, ushered his companions away, and slipped into the stream of bodies before steel or scorn could find them.

At a fork in the road he paused, gauging left and right. Then with a tilt of his chin he led them into Seaborne's opulent depths—always right, for the right road never failed.

At the path's end, they came upon an alehouse bathed in the bright glow of neolyt. Above the door, Sail Ale pulsed in lurid fuchsia, its glow seeping into the night like spilt wine. A prickle of static tingled through Bihan's fingers and toes. He swallowed and stepped forwards, yet the echo of his footfall rang hollow. A glance to either side confirmed the dread truth: he was suddenly, impossibly, alone.

"Easy, mate," came a woman's purr from the shadows. "Hands off those blades. One wrong twitch and my men open your friends' throats."

Her tone was silken, stripped of the guttural bark he'd expect from corsairs. There was a faint lilt instead—an echo of Aledhyn's melting-pot cadence, or perhaps the more northerly ports where bouzoukis sang beneath ancient olive trees.

A chill kiss of steel grazed his spine. He lifted his arms slow as tides. "I'd never have thought a corsair would recognise me," he said. "You keep a library here, I suppose?"

"Three," she replied, twisting the blade just enough for him to feel it. "Our king insists we read before we pillage, so we know what we're dealing with when we cross... aliens. Though the tales never claimed Bihan the Beauty had such a tongue. I always pictured more grunting. Tell me, barbarian," she drew in a sharp breath, "is it true your kind wield steel before you can walk? That you ride beasts before you can even speak?"

Bihan gave a low laugh. "True as any tale you've swallowed. We even test newborns with snakes to see if they'll strangle them or are swallowed whole. Anything can be true, if you want it badly enough."

She stepped into the glow, blade sliding along his flank before resting against his scarred abdomen. A shemagh veiled her face, save for the darkness of her eyes. A strip of gauze bound her bicep, hinting at a fresh wound. Yet what rooted his gaze were the faint, fading henna swirls across her hands and feet. Someone marked by those designs might know where Camila Callo was taken.

"Your friend," she said, nodding towards Rabia, "does she still speak Megaran?"

Bihan turned and froze. Rabia and Shadi knelt in the dirt, knives at their throats.

"That's all?" he scoffed. "You ambush us just to test her tongue and dialect?"

"A warning, actually," she answered, her tone clipped as glass. "Follow me and keep your hands to yourself."

She led them around the alehouse, out onto a tiled balcony overlooking the cove. Two crucifixes loomed in grim symmetry. On one, a youth hung naked, hollow-cheeked, pallid as moonlight. On the other, a dark-skinned man writhed still, "Paladin" carved into his chest. Blood—dried and fresh—streaked the nails through his wrists and ankles, dripping into the mosaic beneath his feet.

Bihan half-drew his dagger, but the steel at Rabia's and Shadi's throats froze his hand.

The woman's laughter—dry as wind over a tomb—drifted through her veil. "Mercy," she said, "is never owed. It's chosen." She circled the crosses. "These two thought themselves greater than clan or kin. The boy dreamt of freedom beyond his mother's hearth and ran. This *Paladin of Wolvesmire* bound himself to a creed across the sea, leaving his own to rot. Both betrayed home for nobler illusions." She caressed the carved letters on the paladin's chest. "By his skin alone, you can guess his birthplace, can't you?"

"Seaborne," Shadi answered first.

Her eyes blazed, fury flaring through her composure before vanishing like a struck match. She snapped her fingers; the magus was gagged, Rabia silenced beside him.

Bihan's throat tightened. "You crucify them... for seeking more?"

"Not for seeking," she said, still as midnight waters. "For hungering beyond their station. Ambition unchecked devours its host. To master it, one must learn how to feed it." Her gaze shifted to Bihan, sharp as a hooked blade. "You chase a girl across seas, cling to friendships older than tides. Fine sentiments. But tell me: when sacrifice demands it, will those chains hold you fast or drown you?"

"I'd never abandon those I love," he said, the words tasting like iron.

Something shadowed her eyes, more than they were. "Noble. But nobility nailed these men here." She tilted her head towards the paladin. "He prized a creed above his kin. I reminded him: every dream carries its price."

She plucked a spear from a hulking corsair at her side. With dancer's grace she drove it into the paladin's ribs. He gave a ragged gasp, defiance bleeding from his face as his body sagged forwards. Silence answered, broken only by the distant call of auctioneers. She wiped the weapon clean against his chest before returning it.

"I'm nothing if not merciful," she said evenly. "Remember my lesson, Bihan. Let go of false loyalties or be prepared to pay the same price."

She clapped once. A rat-faced lieutenant hurried forwards, devotion painted across his features, and shoved Bihan on. The keys at his belt jingled like a bard's bells, each chime mocking Bihan's silence. As they passed the crucifixes, Bihan's eye caught the paladin's swollen, discoloured forearm, and then the title carved into his chest. It was an image that yanked him back to Aledhyn's quayside, to a paladin who'd spoken only of finding his brother, Mathaeus.

* * *

The interior of Sail Ale offered no spectacle, just stout oak tables, low-hung lamps, and a hearth that whispered warmth into the room. Ordinary. And it was precisely the ordinariness Bihan needed. Salted pork, figs, crusty bread, pale ale—meagre comforts, yet comforts nonetheless.

Below the mezzanine, where Bihan sat atop with the shemagh-wearing woman, Shadi and Rabia sat apart, their eyes clinging to him as if he might dissolve into mist at any moment. Torchlight flared across his false eye, each flicker stirring the ghost of those crucified bodies outside, each tingle in his fingers another warning he'd chosen to ignore.

Shadi tugged at his sleeve—a silent reminder of the pearwood wand hidden beneath. Bihan shook his head. Not now. The task was simple: learn Camila Callo's fate, then slip away before curiosity turned to chains. Yet the keys of the rat-faced aide chimed softly behind him, a cruel lullaby reminding him whose ground they stood on.

The woman slid into the chair opposite, kicking her sandalled feet onto the table as though it were her throne. "So," she said, "have you pondered what you saw on the balcony?"

Bihan lifted his mug. Foam trembled like surf atop it. "The paladin crucified for his creed, the boy for freedom. I understand."

"Do you?" A trace of fire flashed in her shadowed eyes before vanishing. She leant closer, veil brushing her cheek. "Then tell me, barbarian, why're you here?"

He set the mug down. His gaze didn't waver. "Camila Callo. Tell me where she is."

Her laughter, soft and girlish, startled in its gentleness. With a languid motion she arched one henna-stained foot, scarlet-painted toes wiggling across the table. "Camila Callo?" she teased. "Never heard of her. Perhaps you've washed into the wrong port."

The sigh of leather marked her sandals sliding free. Bare feet emerged: plump soles dusted with travel, faint grime clinging to their pads, dust gathering beneath the rounded toes. She stretched them into the air, then set them down on the table once more, heels thudding soft against oak. Her insteps curved high, toes spreading and curling with slow indulgence, as though testing the air and lamplight against the faint sweat.

"Or perhaps," she murmured, "I do know Camila Callo... and she simply refuses to know you."

Bihan's gaze caught the henna spirals winding around her toes, motifs familiar from Aledhyn's sūqs. He drew a breath, nodding towards her soles.

"Those designs are Aledhyn work. I know the artist. So, either you've walked the Circular City recently, or you're more than you pretend to be."

Her fingers toyed with the tassels of her shemagh before letting them slip lower, grazing the shallow dip of her cleavage. The poet's blouse shifted with the motion, thin white folds brushing across warm golden skin, clinging for a moment before falling loose again. With a deft tug, the scarf slackened and slid away, the soft rasp of fabric drawing the eye to the sway of her chest beneath. Dirty-blonde curls spilt free across her shoulders. When she looked up, her hazel eyes, one freckled with blue, met his with a knowing spark.

"Camila," he whispered.

"You're perceptive, barbarian." Her toes pressed against his hand, clammy warmth stroking his knuckles. A shiver of heat ran through her skin, damp with the faint sheen of travel. "But it's *Captain Contreras* now, if you please."

Bihan reached for her, a hand at his belt. Her hand slid for her cutlass. In a breath, corsairs hemmed them in. Before steel could sing, the air itself rippled. His false eye convulsed, vibrating with an intensity that made his skull hum. The shimmer split wide, and a Mystic stepped through.

He was olive-skinned, robed in blue and gold, tattoos like serpents curling up his arms. A single eye, glowing faint beneath his hood, caught the room's light. He struck his quarterstaff once, and Rabia and Shadi were teleported to the mezzanine, relief and vigilance clashing in their faces.

The High Mage Montero had arrived.

Calm as ritual, he clasped Shadi's forearm, fingers brushing the outline of the boy's pearwood wand as though greeting an old companion. He turned to Rabia with a courteous nod—then froze at the sight of her horns curving from her forehead. His breath hitched, his chest rose with wonder. Slowly, he bowed, hand pressed over heart in reverence.

Bihan's eye throbbed harder. He couldn't look away. Not from the Mage's shifting tattoos, nor from the way light played along the carved staff. Recognition stirred like an old ache: the leather-bound tome in Shadi's home, the moving illustration he'd pored over. Whether memory or omen, he couldn't tell. Only that his eye pulsed violently in the Mystic's presence, and the question seared him—why did this man now stand before them all, greeting his friends as kin?

With a graceful sweep of his staff, Montero conjured a table laden with fresh fare, chairs unfolding around it: one at the head for Camila, the rest for Bihan, Shadi, and Rabia. Montero stood sentinel at her side, as upright as a drawn blade.

The ordinary alehouse had become a stage. Destinies poised to collide. Bihan slid into his seat, his heart thrumming. Spell or command, he couldn't say. He only knew he was terrified yet eager to see what came next.

X

A Price of Deception

The High Mage's tattooed hands glided along the high back of Camila's chair as though consecrating it, his presence binding meal and conversation alike. His single glowing eye never wavered, pinning Bihan in place. In all his wanderings across the Pocket Globe, he'd never seen a Mystic's gaze burn so unnaturally—save for the killer who razed his childhood home. When pressed, Montero admitted he'd lost the eye long ago to a spell of terrible potency. He refused further explanation, claiming only that the magic left his eye aglow for eternity.

With a formal bow and a hand pressed over his heart, he assured them there was nothing sinister in his magic. Yet a stubborn tingling crept through Bihan's fingertips.

Camila leant forwards then, forcing his hand towards his weapons, and revealed how she'd engineered his arrival in Seaborne from the start. His hunch about her and the stele had proved true, but his chivalry, and his urge to rescue a damsel in distress, had played directly into her grasp. As she spoke, she twirled a lock of blonde hair about a slender finger, her gaze dissecting every ripple in his stance.

Bihan had fulfilled his quest. He'd found Camila Callo. Yet she warned him this wouldn't be the fairy-tale ending inked in adventure novellas. She'd tracked Syrek's last known whereabouts, then ventured to the pyramids, found neither stele nor mummies to slay, and turned instead to the whispers of loyalists who claimed the basalt stele lay in Seaborne. That the corsair captain who'd owned it was docked at Aledhyn's port. Now he was dead, and the antique was hers.

Once she'd chased gold and glory like Bihan the Beauty himself—before Syrek, the stele, and the wyverns veered her course. Since then, her loyalty lay with Toussaint, alongside a host of youths eager to bleed for his crusade. For Al-Qiyamah. She unwound the gauze from her arm and revealed the brand beneath: faintly glowing, Montero's work. Or as he corrected her, *aard*. The iron fist of Clan Toussaint.

"All this to lure me here? Why?" Bihan's voice was low as he leant across the laden table, fingers still poised at his pommels. "Does a simple conversation no longer suffice?"

Montero's reply was smooth as silk. "Because the great Bihan Alihanson would never chase a mere invitation to see his old friend Rabia. I warned Camila of your hesitations, of your dependence on Fregor the Cutpurse. We needed a scheme to draw you both."

The revelation struck him hard. The garnok had been bewitched, Fregor's death twisted to serve a fanatic's plot. His throat locked, words broken against the cage of his teeth.

Shadi slumped lower, wiping damp palms on his trousers. Neither he nor his mother merited more than a passing mention. Each time Bihan pressed, Montero and Camila dismissed them as happy accidents in their design.

"Why me?" Rabia's breath stuttered. Sweat shimmered at her temple. "Why want me above the Beauty?"

Camila's laugh was bright and cutting. "Because you alone read Megaran, true scion of Torbjörn's line. Only you can decipher the stele. Bihan's blade is a trinket, an idol for the masses. Useful, but not essential."

Montero's hand flexed on his quarterstaff, carved wood creaking against the chair's armrest. Bihan knew then the stele was close. They would never abandon it on some mountain or landed ship. Camila's eyes glittered with predatory fire. She'd killed for it. She would again. Rebinding the gauze about her arm, she leant back with languid poise. Bihan's tingling fingers toyed with his hilts. He could smell mutiny in the still air.

"Thus comes the moment where I take what I desire, and the world falls into place. Toussaint will command the wyverns, claim the throne, and restore his iron reign." Her arms swept wide in a grand, theatrical gesture, holding the trio's hungry eyes though none touched a morsel of the elaborate spread. "I meant to present him the stele myself, along with the horned lady khorvo and Bihan the Beauty. Not any-more."

She propped her small feet on the polished wood again, defiance gilding the act. Her blouse slipped open just enough to catch the golden sheen of her skin. Each rise of her chest tested the thin fabric, a quiet show beneath the light. With an idle stretch she scattered crumbs with her plump toes, curling and flexing across bowls of olives and torn bread. Dust smudged the wood where her soles pressed, her henna-stained arches drawing Bihan's gaze as though each line spelt a truth. She caressed the air between them, as though daring him to cross it.

Montero stiffened. The gem atop his staff pulsed fuchsia, tendrils quivering through the wood. His palm clamped the armrest, and his glowing eye dimmed to a hollow abyss.

"Excuse me?" His hiss rolled across the feast like a drawn blade.

The gauze on Camila's arm flared with his fury, a malevolent glow answering the wizard's wrath. She whistled sharply, unfazed. Seizing a pomegranate, she split it in her palms. Seeds spilt like rubies, blood bright against golden skin.

"Join me, Bihan. Together, we can rule this Imperium. With wyverns at our command, we can shatter Toussaint's army and even fell the great dragon. Your legend and my cunning will be celebrated for generations. Your companions will earn high station—"

The table convulsed before her words could land. Platters and goblets crashed as wood collapsed inwards. Camila's legs buckled; she struck the floor with a gasp. Montero's quarter-staff slammed down, splintering boards. Black tendrils burst from the crack, writhing around every foot but his own. Shadi darted forwards, the pearwood wand springing from his sleeve. He loosed a salvo of spells, sparks and cantrips flaring. Montero deflected each with unnerving ease, but the barrage fractured his net of shadow.

In that heartbeat's fracture, Bihan vaulted the wrecked table, blades bared and flashing towards the High Mage.

"Imbecile! I *will not* stand this betrayal!" Montero's roar struck like a hammer. His fingers snapped—and in a sickening jolt, the trio tumbled to the clamouring deck below. "Your loyalty lies with Toussaint!"

Chaos erupted. Corsair blades flashed in the lanternlight. Bihan shoved Rabia clear, steel shrieking as he caught a cutlass on the jagged edge of Alihan's fractured blade. Sparks leapt. He twisted, carving through another assailant before the press swallowed him whole.

Above the fray, Camila applauded with slow, mocking claps. Her grin was cold fire. She spat at the wizard's curly-toed boots before vaulting the rail. Her cutlass gleamed like quicksilver as it slid free of its leather scabbard. She landed before Bihan, shoulders coiled, stance low, eyes hungry.

"Never trust a pyrate," she purred, the words both invitation and threat. The crew melted back, ring widening with expectant silence.

Montero's single eye burnt with wrath as he peered down from above; and then he vanished, leaving only the air's hollow aftertaste.

Camila twirled her cutlass in her palm, the blade a mirror of cruelty. "Are you sure you want this fight? Refuse me, and you'll find no mercy. You remember the crucifixes, right?"

Bihan's lip curled. "Bugger your mercy."

His gaze dropped to her bare feet: the hennaed arches crossing, uncrossing, toes flexing with a dancer's precision. Every step was deliberate, as if her soles carved vows into the boards. She moved with the eerie grace of the Danse Macabre—each shift a promise of violence. The phantom weight of her next step pressed on his nerves before it came.

Rabia broke the tension, tomahawks flashing as she sprang forwards. Bihan pivoted, arm rising to shield her from Camila's cutlass. Tingling surged in his fingers, his toes. No longer a warning he could ignore. He raised his dagger, its familiar heft a vow. Camila slid sideways, cutlass arcing in a hiss that shaved the air from his khopesh. He sprang onto the balls of his feet, blood thundering in his ears.

"Shadi! Shield Rabia. Shield yourself. Whatever magic's left—use it now!"

Corsairs pressed in, faces contorted in savage glee as they chanted: "Pyrate! Pyrate!" Their voices rolled like surf against a storm wall. Camila drank it in, lips curling, arms beckoning them to greater frenzy. Bihan feinted, shoulder dipping, but her smirk never faltered. She knew his rhythm, the tales, the rehearsed flourishes. The sensationalised tomes, however, never mentioned his most barbaric techniques.

With a sudden surge, he vaulted off a burly corsair's chest, dagger thrust straight at the glowing brand on her bicep. She deflected with a deft twist, then kicked the weapon from his hand. It clattered across the floorboards. His lungs burnt.

The tingling spread into a creeping numbness that gnawed at his balance. He raised his khopesh, point aimed at her heart. One stroke could end it. She met it with lazy precision, pivoting on her heel. The blade whistled overhead, severing the ends of her dirty-blonde hair. Camila staggered, fingertips brushing the fallen locks. Her gasp was sharp, her eyes narrowing with possessive fury.

Before he could press the opening, a blunt weight struck the nape of his neck, and fire ripped down his spine. The world collapsed. He crumpled, vision splintering, heartbeat thudding from some distant shore. Rabia and Shadi's cries blurred as corsairs pinned them to the sticky boards.

"Take their weapons. Jail them in the lower quarters," Captain Contreras ordered, voice flat, fingers trailing the gauze at her arm. Her rat-faced aide fumbled keys at her command. "Strip the boy of his wand. Let him keep his greasy parchment—I said weapons, not diary entries. Gag the khorvo. No tongue-biting. We need that stele read. And the barbarian..."

Her hand lingered over the hidden, glowing brand, caressing it like a lover's scar. A silent homage to Montero's lingering magic, and a promise of vengeance yet to come.

Darkness washed across Bihan's vision. Numbness stole his hearing. His final thought flickered like a dying torch:

This can't be the end...

Amid a boundless stage of starless blackness, Bihan dreamt.

He awoke on unfamiliar ground: a desert stretched beneath an ochre sky; its horizon drowned in dust. Bleached titan bones jutted like monuments from the shifting sands, erasing all sense of direction. Each step sank him deeper, the grains clinging like a silent captor. From the heat-haze, a brown bird streaked with grey flecks appeared, mute but steady—an anchor in the void. Drawn by compulsion, Bihan followed.

At the crest of a dune, he beheld them: cloaked apparitions striding in uncanny unison along a knife-edge ridge. A procession without voice or deviation, each clutched a gleaming stiletto, sinewy palms stretched taut around the haft. One by one, they entered the colossal skull of the fallen titan, swallowed whole by its hollow maw until only their vanishing silhouettes remained. Then the sands gave way.

He plunged screaming through blackness, the roar of rushing air swallowing him, until he crashed amid subterranean pillars of oily black matter that glistened with an unsettling light. Illumination leaked from his eye—an unnatural glow. Yet the body he wore stood rigid, gaze fixed on four esoteric doors that pulsed with malignant life before walking through them. He looked down. Tattooed palms, not his own;

hands he'd seen before in nightmare. The Vizier's, or Montero's. In their grasp lay a marble. Across its white surface a black bloom spread, then flared into a perfect fuchsia iris, unblinking.

The dream fractured. Visions assaulted him: thorny roses strewn with severed answers; Syrek's spire looming over a city torn by war; a sacrifice that tore a city from its land; a marble transmuted from pale stone into impenetrable black. His chest seized, breath deserted him. He reached to clutch his heart, but the body refused to move. And then... clarity, brutal and absolute. The glowing eye, the writhing tattoos. Every fragment seared into place: the butcher of Thebes, the hand that murdered his parents, the mage who shifted Syrek itself...

The High Mage Montero *was* Syrek's Vizier.

Rage exploded within him, volcanic, unbearable. His head throbbed to the hammer of his pulse; his dream-body convulsed. Montero's palms warped, tattoos twisting into tendrils, fingers tightening around a phantom throat. His mother's throat. They squeezed.

"No!" Bihan's cry strangled in silence, horror crushing him as the phantom strangulation replayed her death. Tears scalded but gave no release. He writhed helplessly—until memory of himself rose, stubborn and defiant. He remembered his purpose. His will. He forced his eyes shut, denying the dream. Denying Montero. Denying truth itself.

Pain answered.

* * *

The world returned in savage focus: he was bleeding out, suspended above Seaborne's glittering bay. The sea-breeze—once his balm—now carried only the metallic sting of his blood. White-hot agony crackled in every breath. His body hung nailed to splintered timber, not high enough to meet the mezzanine, not low enough to stand. Beside him, a man reeking of piss bore a single word branded across his chest: *Paladin.*

Horror struck like a blade. Crucified.

The word burst from Bihan in a roar that rattled Seaborne's cove. Auctions halted; slaves and slavers alike paled before the wrath that shook the air; a fury Bihan had not unleashed since the Syrek War's bloody end.

Fragments of the dream still seared through him. "Montero!" he bellowed, the name shredding his throat, a savage aria hurled into the night. His cry unravelled to a rasp, leaving only the sick drip of blood, dark pearls pooling around the paladin's shattered form. Above, the moons drifted, pale and indifferent, casting their cold light across the carnage.

He hung crucified by the woman he'd sworn to save. Her mocking smile carved itself into his mind. Above her hovered the Vizier's eye, Montero's eye. Hatred branded him hotter than any wound. If he was free, he'd tear the marble eye from his socket and hurl it into the churning sea. Hosting the cursed object was a defilement beyond flesh.

"I swear it by the life bleeding from my veins," he rasped skywards, throat aflame with conviction. "Those villains will die by my hand! Do you hear me, Seaborne? DEATH COMES!"

Legends say vows forged in such fierce anguish draw divine favour, a spark of old-world magic woven through a warrior's pledge. Bihan's oath blazed with that ancient force. An oath forged in desecration and fury, hurled into the night and carried out upon the tide of undying fury.

XI

A Burden of Bones

In his own mind, Shadimtha Coelho had never known real bravery, nor strength, nor anything to inspire dread. He remained the frightened boy whose palms dampened at the sight of terracotta, a Mystic stunted by every failed cantrip, every spell gone awry. A disappointment to his proud mother, a pitiful fool beside his intrepid brother. Shadi had long since embraced those crushing truths... until he met Bihan the Beauty and spent twelve transformative years in his shadow.

In Bihan, Shadi had come to see the strongest, bravest man alive. Not because of boasts or shining feats, but because he endured—because his presence was enough. At the side of the Last Barbarian, Shadi shed the suffocating labels his family had given him, evolving from a faltering sorcerer into a true magus. It was a gift he'd never found words to thank Bihan for; especially under the gaze of that pure black marble eye, an unsettling relic that seemed always to watch, even when Bihan looked elsewhere.

A chill seeped into his bones. Beside him, Rabia rubbed the persistent ache in her back. Their cell stank of mildew and rust, its stones slick with seepage. Rats nested in what looked disturbingly like a child's ribcage: muscular, yet too small for a grown man. Stripped of weapons and clothing, they shivered in their undergarments. Hugging his knees to his bony chest, Shadi rubbed his arms, finding no warmth—only guilt, thick as the damp that clung to the walls. He felt sure it showed, though if Rabia noticed at all, her pain must have drowned it.

He remembered the way Bihan had studied that marble eye, how his finger tapped against it in a rhythm Shadi couldn't unhear. With each mile closer to Seaborne, where the High Mage Montero held court, the unease had tightened in Shadi's chest. When a magical source neared its rightful owner, it strained against its separation. That knowledge gnawed at him.

He shuddered again as a biting draught snaked through the grate above.

From the forge overhead, a smith hammered without pause, his curses at Captain Contreras striking between each clang of steel. At dawn he'd laughed hoarsely at the sight of two crucified men; by nightfall, only the relentless ring of hammer to anvil broke the silence. Sleep would not come for Shadi or Rabia—pain and chill denied them that refuge.

Shadi prayed Bihan wasn't among the crucified.

He drew the softened parchment from his pocket and read again the spell written there, hearing his mother's voice as though she stood at his shoulder. She'd taught him to act the instant she stole the accursed eye from Montero, along with its incantation. Montero had claimed he learnt it from the Vizier of Syrek, but Shadi had never cared to study evil men and confirm it. He preferred tales of high adventure, of venerable Mystics like the Alpheniq siblings, woven with dragons and valour.

His fingers trembled as they traced the spell. *So close,* he thought. *So close to seeing a wyvern. So close to witnessing dragon-kin.*

Shadi folded the parchment, tucking it back. He doubted he could cast the spell even if he dared. His mother had been adamant: she'd sent him out as an urchin to learn hardship, to understand why her designs mattered. Yet Shadi couldn't justify unleashing the same incantation Syrek's Vizier had loosed all those years ago, only to sate her hunger for dominion over some gothic city he didn't even know how to locate.

"Milddyr asnikt!" Rabia cursed, shaking a fist at the grate that admitted a sliver of pitiless light.

It baffled Shadi that a city so radiant and warm above ground could harbour such frozen cruelty beneath. Seaborne reminded him too much of his mother. Unable to sit still beneath that weight, he paced the length of their cell, testing the hinges with restless hands. He thought of the tales of Bihan's daring escapes from unjust imprisonment, and asked Rabia how they'd managed before. She only winced, shaking her head. Her back throbbed; her eyes clung instead to her twin tomahawks, lying beyond reach beside the crucified paladin's armour.

"Just cast a spell," Rabia grumbled, strained. "Open the lock or something."

"I would if I could," Shadi sighed. "Like you, I'm stripped of my weapon. Without a source, I—"

"Bugger that!" she snapped. "I've seen Mystics cast bare-handed."

"Then you've seen fools, not true Mystics," Shadi answered, heat rising along his chest and neck.

Rabia rolled onto her side, brushing rats from the skeleton's ribs, and pushed herself to her knees. Shadi watched her bend low over the bones, her gaze intense. At first, he saw only bones, but then his eye caught the truth: a khorvo skeleton, tall-horned and stout, its bones thicker than any human's. No armour remained, no name.

Rabia leant close, so near the rats shrank away. She traced the horns—so like her own—with her thick fingers and followed the remnant's ridges down to the hips. A soft giggle escaped her lips: surprising, almost tender. Her eyes gleamed. She pointed first to the horns, then at Shadi, laughing again in a low and knowing tone.

"The hips, Shadi," she whispered, spittle clinging to her dark lips, "broader than a male's, wouldn't you say?"

Shadi stepped closer, studying as memory returned. Lessons in anatomy with Montero. The pelvis flared wider, the iliac crest less pronounced. Undeniably female. Yet the horns were broad, ridged, masculine. Just like Rabia's. His breath caught. Only one other female khorvo with such horns had crossed their path in all his travels. The same horns he'd seen catch Bihan's ankles in Syrek.

"Torbjörn?" he breathed. Rabia's nod was sharp, certain. "They held her here. Captured her. This must've been before Camila. Montero, then... Montero did this."

Rabia traced Freja's horns, then her own, noting how both curved at the tips and undulated along the midshaft. "However they trapped this warrior, she never yielded. She refused to translate the stele. Why else call on me? She died here, in this pit, for that stubborn silence. Neither axe nor sword could cleave her, but the damp claimed her life. A hero of legend, left to rot unburied."

Shadi laid a hand on Rabia's shoulder, his words hushed. "She died protecting the wyverns."

Rabia's gaze hardened. She rose, her frame suddenly vast in the narrow space. "An honourable end. If we escape, we must never let that stele fall to other hands. We can't allow it to be read. I don't know what's on your parchment, nor do I care to know. All I need from you now is a promise, even if it costs me my life."

The demand staggered him against the bars. Shadi loathed promises. Every broken oath weighed like a millstone on his soul: the vow to his mother, the spell he'd yet to cast. He would do anything to keep Rabia safe, but promises...

She seized his wrists, her grip unnervingly strong, drawing him forwards until his chest brushed hers. "Promise me," she said, insistent as iron.

His heart pounded so hard it rattled his slender limbs. He glanced at Freja's remains and, for a moment, saw Rabia's bones in their place. He shuddered. The dungeon stank of rot; overhead, the smith's hammer fell again, each clang echoing through his skull. Rabia held him silent, her small, sharp eyes boring into him as if to pierce his soul. If she died because of him—because of this promise—would Bihan ever forgive? Could he? The thought of orphaning her children and widowing her spouse pressed against his chest like a slab of stone.

He drew a ragged breath. "I promise," he whispered.

The words sparked in his mind like a barn catching flame. A reckless idea leapt to life, tempered at once by the realisation that he *still* wielded no wand. Rabia caught his shift and pressed him to explain. Shadi blurted it out: if they worked a spell on the remains, they could summon Freja's spirit and force from her lips the stele's hiding place. Surely the corsairs had dragged her to it repeatedly, trying to break her silence.

Convincing Rabia was easy. Convincing himself took far longer. Because even though the plan was sound, brilliant even... it was dangerous. Necromancy was the one discipline Basem at Spellforge had forbidden him, and yet he'd dabbled anyway, unable to resist. It wasn't stigma that stayed his hand now, but the lack of a source. That was why they still rotted in this cell. Memory carried him back to his first journey with Rabia and Bihan, the day an ancient manticore demanded sacrifice beside a pumpjack. He would've given himself up, had they not intervened. He owed them both too much.

"I'll do it," he said, breath ragged, "but once she rises, you must ask your questions quickly. Precise. No stories, no lingering. I'm sorry if that sounds harsh—I'm only... nervous."

"Don't be," Rabia said, her mouth curving into a reassuring smile. "You'll do great."

He swallowed hard, staring at his fingertips, already feeling the searing pain where scars would form, as he braced for the spell. Rabia stepped back to the wall, leaving him space. He summoned the incantation from memory and recalled the dark invocation he'd whispered only once before, although incompletely. Spirits, he knew, responded well to words spoken aloud and clearly.

"Once born, once dead; return to us, Freja Torbjörn, and speak in my stead!"

Verdant sparks gushed from his fingertips, drifting like fireflies before sinking into the bones and the sand-strewn floor. A ring of pallid toadstools erupted, encircling the remains. They shimmered faintly, quaffing magic through unseen roots. One by one, the mushrooms bloomed—not the blood-red of natural growth, but a sickly green, anticlockwise.

Above Freja's skull, the final toadstool pulsed, and in the circle's heart a pentagram coalesced, its five points anchored by throbbing fungi.

It had begun. Cold seized him. Not the fleeting bite of winter air, but a profound, marrow-deep chill that climbed from his ankles like shackles of ice. It crept inexorably up-wards, thick and unyielding, until it reached his gaping mouth, frozen open in silent horror. The chamber itself seemed to listen; motes stilled in the dawn's light, suspended mid-drift. A low moan swelled from the stones, and then that glacial breath forced itself into his throat—like drinking ice water under a merciless sun, bitter and endless, chilling him to the soul.

He tried to speak, but his voice died strangled. His lips trembled, and when they parted, it wasn't his words that spilt out but the ragged whisper of another.

"Why... summon me back... why here?" Freja rasped, her voice tearing through him in fractured syllables.

Rabia's tears caught the new light. Sorrow battled her fierce resolve as she leant close, her voice breaking with ur-gency. "Answer me, General Torbjörn. Why were you kept here? Where's your stele? Help me protect the wyverns."

Shadi's hand blazed with torment as Freja forced her tale through him. "Captured... dragged to an alehouse. Interro-gated by... an old friend. One-eyed." Each word tore like glass through his veins. "Buried within Syrek. Underground... city returned. Find the vault... find the stele. My kin... protect the wyverns... at all costs. Montero... never control... never."

"Syrek?" Rabia's whisper drifted towards the brittle bones at her feet. She bowed her head, reverent. "I'll guard your se-crets, General."

Peace, or something near to it, settled over the skeleton. But the air still reeked of burning flesh, and magic's toll spread across Shadi's charred skin. A burgundy stain crept up his wrist and forearm, pulsing with each fresh wave of agony. His head pounded with relentless rhythm, and hoarse, raw cries tore from his throat. He'd held the spell too long. Yet amid the torment, he clung to the thought: his debt to his friends was paid.

Rabia froze, panic etched into her face, her fingers hovering helplessly as though touch alone might soothe the storm raging through him. He endured. Seconds fractured into shards of agony, each heartbeat an eternity. This was the price. Magic's laws were forged in ages past, immutable and unyielding, binding every magus who followed their path, and they were destined to outlast all generations.

Then stillness—sudden, absolute. The tempest broke, leaving only the dull hammer of pain behind his eyes. The cell wheeled about him like the whirling dervish his mother once rode. He winced at the memory of her then: stoic as each burgundy tattoo was carved into her skin, never flinching, never weeping. A sorceress who bowed to no coven, acknowledged no authority. Her only crime was independence, and she paid it in suffering. Shadimtha had chosen another path, but the ache was no less profound.

When his thoughts finally stilled, he lay his head against Rabia's shoulder—then a convulsion seized him. He lurched forwards and expelled not blood, not bile, but a clotted black sludge that stank of the grave. Ectoplasm. The taste clung bitter on his lips, a ghastly echo of Freja's brief possession. And then came the crawling. A legion of invisible slugs seemed to writhe up from his gut, slithering through his throat to spill from his mouth, leaving their slick, nauseating trail behind.

"Wicked," he murmured, with a half-delirious grin. Then blackness fell, and he surrendered to oblivion.

When Shadi awoke, he didn't at first know himself. He sat astride a bay mare in the heart of an endless desert, clad in armour he'd only glimpsed once—locked behind Darragh's glass cabinet. Behind him dragged a basalt stele, its bulk furrowing the dunes with the same grim grace the *Delphine* carved into the Shamrock Sea. By the horned shadow cast across the sand, he knew: this was not his body.

He fumbled beneath his sleeve for his wand. Only raw scars burnt his palm. Two battle-axes, hafts dark with old blood, hung at his saddle, their knotwork echoing the Megaran arches of Aledhyn. He dared not speak. Fear sealed his tongue.

Hour by hour the mare pressed forwards, hooves sinking deep under the weight of relic and rider. He glanced at blood-caked wrists and felt a regret not his own—a sorrow for fleeing battle to guard creatures unnamed. Then came the whisper: *What creatures? Wyverns?* His chest constricted. The memories did not belong to him.

They were Freja's.

Through her, he tasted betrayal: a friend turned megalomaniac, a forbidden spell scrawled on fragile parchment, a war twisted. She had condemned innocents to rot in eternity beside the horrors Montero concealed from the patriarch in the Tomahawk Prince's quarters. Only a handful had slipped the grand spell, and she clung to the hope their end was swift, merciful. That hope, bitter as sand, was the only grace she allowed herself. And so, she wandered aimlessly in an endless atonement across arid lands, driven by the quiet conviction that such sacrifice alone served the greater good.

The desert was her judge and jailer.

From the haze of a steppe, a figure coalesced: a robed man in crushed-berry hues—amaranth—eyes glacial with mirth, and a parchment staff humming with magic. *Aard*, Montero would have called the old craft. His voice was older still, and he spoke in an alien language. When the stranger shifted into Common, the timbre curled through memories that pulsed within both Shadi and Freja's blood like a bell. This wanderer of dunes was Basem Alpheniq of Spellforge.

Scars scored his flesh in burgundy sigils, burnt deep into neck and forearms. He looked half kin to Montero's plague-ravaged visage, and Freja shuddered. Desperation drove her plea: the path to Ophir, so she might lay her relic to rest in the grand city of her ancestors. Alpheniq smiled thin as a knife, moustache twisting, and bent close, his breath hot as desert wind, and hissed his warning: abandon the stele and destroy it.

Her hand trembled on the reins. She would not.

She rode on. Days dissolved under a pitiless sun. Thirst clawed her throat raw, her armour gnawed at her shoulders, every sinew ached with fire. A doe appeared on the dunes—frail as a mirage, hunger mirrored in its eyes. She spurred the mare into a gallop, sure that it was a trick. They thundered past spiders the size of boars, their glossy shells half-buried in loess, past banditos crouched by smothered fires, past the red spires of Thebes stabbing skywards in silence.

Corpses littered the sand, old comrades from Syrek, sun-bleached and abandoned. Her pulse faltered. How long had she wandered? She looked back—the stele still dragged, chained and scraping, her constant companion. Death itself followed like a rancid shadow.

Years bled into each other. The mare perished; a camel bore her burden. When it stumbled, a stallion took its place. Every dawn she woke to the same grim task: the stele's weight, its inscription unread, its burden unshared.

At last, when her body bowed beneath the armour and her spirit scraped against despair, she let her weight fall against the stallion's neck. She expected silence. Instead, she heard a brook's laughter, the mournful creak of boughs, an owl's lonely call. She opened her eyes. Damp air filled her lungs, heavy with cinnamon and smoke. A rainforest pressed close around her, leaves thick as shields, emerald dripping with rain. After the desert's decree, here life thrived unyielding.

On her left, arboreal spires rose as tall as Syrek's towers, their crowns bound by draped vines where monkeys swung and shrieked in the dim canopy. To her right, stone monoliths loomed like tombstones, silent memorials casting shadows across her path. Beneath her, the stallion plunged into a stream so clear it seemed suspended on air, its surface flecked with motes of magenta light that separated darting minnows from tadpoles. Magic made visible.

Beyond the bank, mossy stones lay in orderly rows, each crowned by an ancient tree whose twisted trunk curved into the likeness of a vase. Faces were carved into the bark, familiar and accusing, lips parted in eternal rebuke: *Why did you leave us?*

She slid from the saddle, abandoned her armour, unbuckled the stele, and dragged its weight onto her shoulders. Her breath broke into quick, stabbing bursts. The forest pressed close, fever-thick. From above came a creak—not monkeys. A resonant howl rolled through the undergrowth. Wolves. Fear drove her onwards, yet curiosity urged her deeper until she stumbled into a glade where bodies floated belly-up in the stream, ankles shackled to the depths. Others hung in rusted cages, their skin green with moss and dripping dew.

A cemetery. Lush, haunting, but alive with grief that seeped from the earth itself.

She ran, branches lashing her cheeks. The corpses followed, pressing closer until the world collapsed into blur. When the pounding in her chest slowed, she stood once more in Syrek. But the city was drowned in shadow: its ramparts slick with an oily sheen, its beauty corrupted. Before her rose a statue—towering, divine—the very idol Montero worshipped. Its glistening surface seemed to breathe, and its gaze pierced her as molten steel. Apparitions writhed at its feet: cloaked figures from the Tomahawk Prince's quarters, their eyes burning with accusation. The horrors had survived and she had been captured.

Her chest knotted with guilt. Where were those she'd abandoned? And who, even now, still hunted the stele's translation? Not the Vizier—he'd shed that name. The High Mage. He'd pursued her for years, across deserts, across dream and ruin... and now he had her. Every day he dragged her before the idol, demanding she unlock the stele's secrets. Every day she refused. And so, a cell swallowed her—damp, bare, lightless—visited only by Montero himself. Never food. Never water.

Survived, barely, on the refrain that echoed through her skull: *Protect. Protect. Protect.*

When her body failed, the stele's burden lived on. She had died to deny Montero its words and the whereabouts of the wyverns, bequeathing the oath to her kin.

Shadi jerked awake. Rabia's arms slipped as he crashed against the iron bars, lungs burning with remembered desert heat and Syrek's shadows. He *knew* now where the stele lay: a Seaborne vault, a chasm, the subterranean remains of the gothic city.

Nausea ripped through him. He gagged, and a fountain of ectoplasm spilt from his throat, coating Freja's bleached bones and the withered toadstools. Then all of it—bone, fungus, spectral rot—sank into the shifting sand, leaving only silence.

XII

A Promise Forged in Blood

As the moons drowned beneath the horizon, dawn crept across the crucifixion, brushing its pallid light against the withered flesh of two men. Bihan the Beauty wrenched his left hand free from the rusted nail that transfixed it. Skin split; muscle coiled; nerves shrieked on the iron's serrated bite—an echo of a bard plucking a macabre chord from a fleshy mandolin.

His cry tore the silence, a ragged roar that rattled the ribs of the earth. Bile surged through his throat, spilling over his chest and the mosaic beneath. Its acrid stench tangled with the rank reek of Mathaeus' waste, yesterday's vomit, and the copper tang of blood. In that filth, freedom bled its first taste.

The world canted, as though Seaborne itself had been cast on loaded dice by some careless divine. His left hand trembled uselessly, fingers quivering whenever he willed them shut. Beside him Mathaeus sagged, breaths shallow, a husk hovering near death's edge. Bihan's gaze, however, lingered on his mangled hand, memorising the cruel motion it'd taken to tear it free, and abandoned the thought of doing it again.

The ruin mocked him... but a savage notion flared. He lifted the bloodied stub to his mouth and bit deep, imagining roasted meat instead of his own flesh. As his teeth sank through bruised skin, a violent surge of sensation shot up his forearm, rattled through his bicep, and thundered into his heart. His pulse boomed; numb digits twitched awake. He clenched them into a fist and, bracing against the tremor, slammed that fist onto the nail pinning his other hand. Fingers slick with his own gore clawed at the shaft, slipping, failing, until rage overcame restraint and blurred his vision.

"Come on, you bastard," he snarled, tearing with every shred of strength. The nail groaned, shrieked against bone, then came loose, clattering to tile before vanishing in the muck.

Brother Mathaeus jerked awake, lifting his sharp-boned face, eyes narrowing at the veiny ruin and discolouration of his forearm. *Why there?* Bihan wondered, even as his own agony roared fresh. Yet this second release of flesh had spared him the searing agony of the first. Clenching his right hand, he seized the spike in his ankle, twisting. To his surprise, the iron slid clean, like a blade from water.

His weight collapsed forwards, and he struck the mosaic in a slick baptism of bile and blood. His limbs quivered, his nerves fizzled in uncertain silence, and the peculiar tingling ebbed. *Would the sensation ever return?* Mathaeus' lips twitched into a deathly smirk, similar to Montero's. Rage motivated Bihan. Vengeance steadied him. He pressed slick fingers to the glass orb embedded in his skull and dug hard, tearing skin, pulling until ribbons of red wept down his face. The orb shifted, resisted, then hummed with fuchsia sparks and locked back into place, defiant as ever.

A rasp carried behind him, quieter than birdsong. "Ma... mag..."

Bihan turned. His eye trailed from Mathaeus' blood-smeared feet to the crude carving in his chest. "Magic?" he croaked. "I know."

The paladin wheezed. "No. You... don't. Free me." His lips cracked; his words clung to life. "I know where they keep your friends. Don't leave me. Free me, and I'll guide you."

Bihan's good eye flickered as he weighed his options. The keys lay with Camila's rat-faced quartermaster, but the jail's location remained a mystery. Caring for Mathaeus would cripple his flight; yet wandering wounded and weaponless might kill them both. With only a heartbeat's hesitation, Bihan wrenched the nails from Mathaeus' limbs, the paladin slumping free, kicking away those metal thorns. Blood pooled at his feet. Then, with slow deliberation, Mathaeus took the nail that'd pinned his ankles from the barbarian's shivering palm and opened his own discoloured forearm. From the wound he pulled a tiny phial, golden liquid gleaming like sunrise on black water.

He drained it to a single drop. At once his blood—old and fresh—drew along the crucifix and tiles as though beckoned by unseen hands. His dark skin smoothed, wounds knitting to scars, until only old battles and the word "Paladin" marked him.

He turned, offering the phial to Bihan. "One drop, barbarian, and your wounds will close. Only my order may drink deep, but to share even this much is an honour. I owe you that." His hand lifted to Bihan's jaw, guiding the glass to his lips. "Now, drink, and know the blessing of our divine."

He parted cracked lips and let the phial's rim brush his tongue. A sheening smear of the paladin's saliva—metallic with blood—slicked his tastebuds, then the last drop of golden elixir slid home. It struck like cold fire, fizzing across his tongue before plunging down his throat. Tremors raced through him, a staccato of sensation that skittered from muscle to marrow. His belly clenched in a bright, violent knot, then emptied as if some invisible hand had struck peace into him.

Agony fell away like cast-off skin. Flesh knitted, nerves reattached to their cords, blood returned to channels he'd thought dead. Little motes of light rose from the tiles and threaded into his pores. In the dawn's pale wash the world snapped sharper, colours sharpening like lenses focused.

Bihan held out his right hand and watched. Bones realigned, scar tissue smoothed, but the wound through his left hand refused to vanish—unhealed. Each attempt at a fist ended half-formed, fingers stalling like an engine that wouldn't bite. He flexed and released, tasting a new, bitter grief for dexterities lost and for the cost paid to pry them free.

Beneath the hum of returning ichor, something else moved. The marble in his skull scratched—a thin, merciless rasp—like an insect under his skin. For a fevered instant he fancied the divine current would wrench it out. Divinity, the oldest and truest magic, had raged through him; the elixir's fire had answered. He pressed a palm to the glass as if will alone might force it to obey the holy essence. The orb quivered, hummed, crackled... then stilled. The scratch became a private torment, a pinch at a nerve that wouldn't abate.

Bihan swallowed disappointment as a bitter draught. The scratch in his socket now a taunting whisper of defeat. He'd felt the surge of celestial fire, the luminescent tendrils racing through his veins, yet Montero's eye remained lodged, its glassy surface unyielding to holy will.

He clenched a fist, his raw knuckles pressing into his palm. All that power, distilled and divine, had failed to pry Montero's essence from his flesh and repair his self-imposed wound. But he was able to walk; he was able to stand upright thanks to the divinity. And then, through the lingering blackness in his left vision, he made out two words scored into the orb's back. The same cryptic syllables he'd seen on the gnat's greasy scrap of parchment. The spell.

"I'm not much for faith," he rasped, knuckling the marble as the letters bobbed at the edge of thought. "But... bugger me sideways if that wasn't a miracle."

Mathaeus clapped a scarred hand on his shoulder. The paladin swayed, then offered a greeting borrowed from another age, stiff with ritual. "Sir Mathaeus D'Laurentice of Criphollow, at your service."

Bihan returned the old-world salutation, clasping forearms and shaking once in the solemn, confident way men used before battle. "Bihan Alihanson of Thebes." He inclined his head. "Before sunlight bleeds into our cover of darkness... let's find that rat-faced bastard with the keys."

Inside the Sail Ale, Bihan hugged the sticky floorboards, a shadow in a room that stank of stale wine and old urine. Night's breath clung to the corners where shutters still muted the dawn. He and Mathaeus shared a pint of water from the bar and crept towards the mezzanine. Bihan paused at each doorway, thoughts measured and low. Contreras would be where her quartermaster hid; the squalor downstairs hinted she'd retreated upwards to her quarters tidy enough to polish toenails rather than trench with her crew.

He led the way, every step a small calculation.

Unarmed and denuded of armour, they were exposed before a crew that would sell their mothers for a pint. Yet that very vulnerability worked for them. Mathaeus' newly healed limbs moved without the clank of metal; each step swallowed by the stairwell's hush. Even the boards, still warm with the residue of Montero's spell, refused to complain. Courtesy of the corsair king, and Bihan found himself oddly grateful.

At the mezzanine's top the rat-faced guard slumped against a dull blue door, drool pooling on his belt above a jangling ring of keys. He was a pathetic barrier between Bihan and what came next. Bihan could slip through shadows like smoke, but close-quarters theft cramped him; Rabia would've been perfect here, light fingers and a thief's calm. But in the hush of dawn, Bihan alone must play the thief.

A fresh draught skittered along his spine and for a savage instant his mind offered a bloody solution: slit the wretch's throat, watch him choke on his own life. The taste of retribution was sweet and immediate. He kept silent, every muscle coiled for violence.

"Stay," he hissed at Mathaeus. "Watch the stairs."

He slid across the sticky floor, skirting scorch-marks and flicking aside the guard's boot to reveal a kitchen knife, the blade smeared with dried apple juice rather than blood. Not a warrior's steel, yet honest enough. His left hand flexed; the fingers twitched like broken spokes but faltered halfway, buckling into a half-curled claw. Sweat trickled down his forearm as the stained wood rasped along his calluses. He swapped the blade into his right hand and clenched it until the knuckles blanched.

Rage crested—hot, uncompromising. He pictured Rabia's aching spine—the cell floors would be a cruel bed for any spine—Shadi's despair behind bars, the poxy wizard Montero's smirk, and Captain Contreras nailing him to a crucifix. The knife felt right in his fist, hungry. He approached, each footstep a silent vow. The rat-faced man stirred, keys jangling.

Bihan breathed, cold and hard, and came close. There would be no mercy, only the swift justice of blood for blood.

A single sweep across the hamstring and the rat-faced man crashed into Bihan's waiting arms, a strangled cry choked by thick fingers clamped over his mouth. The blade hovered above a crooked nose, tremor in the man's sobs drawing it closer. Silence promised itself in the glint of steel.

"Show me the key to the cells," Bihan growled. The guard's shaking finger found the rustiest iron on his belt and pointed. "Now. Your captain's room."

Tears filled the man's eyes. He shook his head. Bihan pressed the serrated edge against his jugular, nostrils flaring at the stench of fear. Releasing his claw-like grip on the pyrate's mouth, Bihan urged him to whisper with only a look that needed no words.

"Only she has that key," the man whimpered. "I swear."

Bihan hauled him upright and edged to the peephole carved in the door by some voyeuristic impulse. The bite of morning air carried the faint scent of jasmine and sweat as he peered inside.

White satin sheets pooled beneath a sleeping silhouette: Camila Callo Contreras, her golden skin aglow in the thin wash of dawn. Strands of hair clung to her shoulders, soft as dust against the curve of her back. The sheet slipped low, cupping the swell of her hips and the generous rise of her bottom, abundant and inviting even in stillness. Her feet, once dust-stained, now bore the faintest tint of orange on her high-arched soles and toes; warm and clammy, he imagined.

She looked serene, a vision of rippling curves and sun-lit flesh, her body a study in temptation draped across the bed. Yet peace was only surface: beauty couldn't scrub the corruption coiled within. Still, he watched—he couldn't help it. His eye lingered on every hollow, every soft rise and fall, hunger and revulsion braided together so tight he couldn't tell which led the charge.

He let his gaze sweep the chamber, and it greeted him with a disquieting abundance: a burnished mahogany table was strewn with Muzali amulets, silver reliquaries and painted icons. Once, such tokens might've seemed holy; now, under the hush of dawn and the shadow of her naked form, they felt almost profane, relics turned accomplices to temptation, trinkets brandishing piety while hiding rot.

Muzali doctrine, he knew, mirrored the Paladins' own creed they swore their swords to. As with the khorvo and their Great Smith, whose tenets sprang from the same bedrock as the Realm's dominant church. These tokens, however, meant nothing beside the hypocrisy of the woman who crucified him.

Resolve steeled him. He'd take her head. But the key she guarded alone kept that vengeance hovering perpetually out of reach.

He returned to the guard and, without a second's hesitation, dragged the knife across the quartermaster's scrawny throat. Bihan watched crimson geyser over the blue door, splashing hot across his chest and pooling beneath his bare feet. The rat-faced man sagged into his arms, gurgled once, twice, then stilled. His jaw dropped open in a last, everlasting silence.

Mathaeus watched with eyes wide as a child and old as ruin. Awe and revulsion warred across his features. Bihan's breath came shallow. This kill was only the first blow in the chain—next, he'd storm the dungeons and tear his friends from their chains before the sun had fully climbed.

Keys warm in his fist, they moved through streets emptied of morning bustle, skirting the mana-lamps still dim with amber glow. Each footstep echoed against shuttered windows and sleeping cobbles as Bihan steered Mathaeus into a narrow alley beneath a sycamore, its boughs heavy with dew and leaves greener than the sea he'd sailed.

A low drone of commerce drifted towards them: mongers unpacking glittering crayfish, bulging sacks of sugar slumping open, barrels of plundered rum, chains clinking against iron slave collars. In that half-light of dawn, their footsteps muted, they were invisible.

"You'd no right," Mathaeus hissed, eyes fixed on the clotted red under Bihan's rough nails. His voice trembled with an ugly restraint. "No right to take his life."

Bihan flexed his hand, dried blood tugging at his skin. "I'd every right."

"He gave you what you wanted, barbarian." Mathaeus' jaw clenched; his voice wavered between disgust and restraint. "I won't sanctify murder."

"I've not asked for sanctity," Bihan muttered. "Just shut your holy mouth and lead the way."

Mathaeus' lip curled. "Animal." He shouldered past and took point, steel in his stride.

The word bit deeper than any blade.

Bihan's chest tightened, a dull ache spreading as he watched the knight's back retreat into shadow. He'd torn this man down from his crucifixion, wrenched him from death itself, and still the thanks was a slur spat like venom. A zealot hypocrite entrenched in vows and prayer, the paladin hunted Mystics with holy zeal yet now passed judgement on a man whom he owed his life to.

"We're close," Mathaeus whispered, pressing Bihan against the corrugated iron of a shed. A corsair staggered into the street, grunting as he pissed brazenly against a post before slumping asleep where he stood. "Once we pass the smith, we'll press a feigned authority on the jailers."

Bihan's skin prickled as he appraised their nakedness. "Bit difficult," he said, jabbing a thick finger at Mathaeus' breastbone. "Your occupation's written all over you."

For the first time the knight's mouth curled—half sneer, half rueful grin. "I've a plan. It'll work."

"In the nude?"

Mathaeus gave a small shrug, eyes glinting pale green in the guttering light. "What better time to show raw talent than when we're at our rawest?" He nodded down the alley. The corsair had collapsed in his own filth, dead to the world.

Orange-grey clouds churned overhead. Sunlight bled through gaps in chimneys and awnings, painting hard streaks across alleyways. They crossed a rickety plank bridge above a brook that hissed and bubbled, then crouched behind the coarse bark of a maple. The smith's hammer rang ahead, each strike sparking against steel, each plume of smoke bitter with iron. The air reeked of metal, suffocating in its weight. Bihan knew this rhythm too well: a forge pressed into war, spitting out weapons fit for peasants and raiders alike—not the polished pride of knightly swords.

The thought soured in Bihan's gut. Camila Callo had once chased tales of him, hungering for adventure. He remembered Muam Al-Dyn, the desperate name he'd murmured to Rabia—a hope for an end to bloodshed and battlefields. Yet what'd that hope birthed? More graves. More children pressing cheap blades or familial relics to little chests. Legends twisted into funerals. How many had died chasing a fable they didn't fully understand? How many died for someone else's war?

A hand settled on his shoulder, thick and calloused, drawing him back. "What gnaws at you, barbarian?" Mathaeus' voice softened, almost gentle. "In times like this, a prayer steadies the heart and stomach."

Bihan met his gaze. "Not today."

Rust-specked swords hung from the weather-worn rafters above the smith's head; his maker's marks etched like meaningless scratches. But fresh blades bore the clenched iron fist of Toussaint. Contreras no longer served that tyrant—her mark would come soon enough. Her crew's loyalty belonged to her, forged in flame and blood, not in oaths to mages or kings. Montero could weave his spells, but his hand was not the city's law, and he remained an outsider.

Bihan's eye found the iron grates that breathed stale air into the dungeon below. Rabia and Shadi squatted in those shadows beyond. Once freed, vengeance could begin. Fingers tightening around the rotten haft of his stolen knife, he watched the smith's hulking silhouette through smoke and sparks.

With a single step, he moved to prise another cog from the grinding wheel of war.

XIII

A Debt of Blood and Iron

Bihan's feet sank into damp earth as he lunged for the smith's throat. Mould and hot metal curled in his nostrils, each breath tasting of iron and ruin. The forge's light trembled against his blade until a scarred ebony hand arrested its arc. Pale-green eyes, ringed with lashes dark as coal, met his. There was no plea in them, no threat, just a thin, aching thing that pressed against Bihan's ribs. His fingers eased from the mouldy hilt.

Mathaeus stepped through the forge haze, every muscle bound and ready. He laid a palm on the smith's shoulder; the man turned, confusion softening into the slow betrayal of surprise. Then Mathaeus drove the blade home. Flesh split in wet, red arcs. Bihan's heart hammered as the smith sank to one knee, the knife flicking between ribs and neck, pulling crimson ribbons with each stroke. The final thrust stilled him. Mathaeus sagged across the corpse and breathed raggedly, spent.

Blood seeped into the dirt, a dark, living mud where motes and stray moths might one day land.

Bihan crouched beside him, fingertips brushing warm blood. "'Animal,' was it? That's what you called me." The name still tasted like salt and old shame.

Mathaeus pushed himself up, legs uncertain, and cast the knife aside as if it were spent iron. He pressed a hand to his chest and exhaled until his ribs moved. "He deserved it," he said. The words weighed like stone.

Bihan's pulse thrummed in his ears. "Why?" he asked.

Mathaeus' eyes went distant. From beneath the smith's oil-dark apron he drew a small, crested brooch and pressed it to his breast until his knuckles whitened. Only then did he nod. "Let's move, barbarian."

They descended into the jail's belly. Damp walls dripped; every footstep answered them with an echo. Two jailers slumbered in the gloom: one draped over a longbow, the other bent over a miniature carrack. Cyan sails strained on the tiny ship, the *Delphine's* golden crest at its masthead. Each sail bore fine inked instructions, scrawled directly onto canvas as though the builder feared losing a single scrap of guidance.

Bihan studied the toy with a practised eye. Obsession etched into every painted plank. "Camila's handiwork?"

Mathaeus offered a ghost of a smile. "She plans with toys. We follow with steel."

They turned into darker corridors. Night seemed to hold its breath around them, full of promise and old debts.

Sir Mathaeus then took the lead and strode towards the jailers with the same fierce swagger that'd carried him through the smithy, naked flesh marred by drying blood gleaming in lamplight. He presented the brooch to the jailer crouched over the model ship. The jailer lifted the crest, brought it to his mana-lamp, and with a weary sigh surrendered. He returned the brooch, inclined his head, and opened the way.

Mathaeus' pale-green eyes flashed, satisfied.

"Lead on," Bihan said.

Torchlight swallowed lamplight as they threaded through cell after empty cell. Each barred room was a mute testament to forgotten cruelties—rotted corpses, skeletal remains half-swallowed by moss and mildew. Deeper still, voices teased the dark. One tone, honeyed and urgent, slithered down the corridor, weaving through air thick with the scent of orange-tree blossoms, tomato paste, and rosemary. Faint tangs of wet coins, too. *Rabia.* Bihan broke into a sprint, lungs burning, and found her kneeling beside Shadi. The boy shivered, head in her lap, fingertips tracking the jagged burgundy sigils that crawled along his forearm and hand.

Bihan dropped beside them. "You cast without your wand, didn't you?" They were a mirror of the markings Shadi's mother bore. "Basem warned you."

Shadi offered a crooked grin, breath ragged. "He warned me not to dabble in necromancy, too. He also taught me not to ignore a debt. A friend of yours?" His gaze slid to Mathaeus as the paladin crouched to adjust the straps to his reclaimed armour.

Bihan tapped his marble with a thumb. "Questions first. Answers after." The orb hummed under his touch.

Rabia's hand came down, iron-sure. "First, kilt on," she ordered. "Get us out of here before Camila wakes. No dawdling. No speeches. We leave now or this rescue fails."

In the tales they whispered of Bihan Alihanson, this was the moment he would seize the bars with fingers like iron hooks and tear them apart, carving a tunnel to freedom for his starving companions. But no such myth took shape then. Instead, he slipped the stolen key into the rusted lock and turned it with a single, decisive click. The door swung wide. Torchlight flared across weary faces as they dressed, tore at bread and jerky, and stitched together the story of their captivity—each voice a different thread, weaving the tapestry of their ordeal anew.

Sir Mathaeus kept apart, gilt longsword balanced on his shoulder, his warnings falling like hammer blows: their time was borrowed, the city would soon rouse, corsairs would swarm the streets. Bihan let those cautions drift around him like ash. He savoured the scraps of their stories: the flare of Rabia's memory, the clipped, deliberate precision in Shadi's retelling—because their revelations shook him to the marrow. The stele was here in Seaborne. Syrek lay entombed beneath its stones.

Each confession struck him like a mallet, until words deserted him and his hands moved instead, buckling straps and weighing blades. But then his left hand betrayed him; the mangled fingers locked in their crooked half-claw, incapable of closing round the dagger's grip. He forced the steel into his right, every swing awkward, unbalanced. His khopesh—the weapon sung of by bards—lay untouched among the heap of discarded arms. If vengeance for Montero's treachery was to be wrought, it would be with this dagger: the very steel that splintered on the day Thebes was lost.

"Bihan?" Rabia thrust her tomahawks towards him, edges gleaming. "We're ready. What now?"

He swallowed. "We find the stele. But first, Shadi, this marble in my skull—"

"I can't remove it," Shadi cut in, sliding his pearwood wand into his sleeve. He brushed back a wisp of hair and squared his shoulders. "It's bonded to you. You tried at the crucifixes, and nothing happened, right?"

Sir Mathaeus stepped closer, pinning the looted brooch to his shoulder cape in a gesture both grave and proud. "Your magic can undo it, young Mystic," he said, almost goading. His pale-green eyes held Shadi's, unblinking.

Rabia prowled the chamber, jaw clenched, her movements taut as a wolf in a cage. "Why the pomp, Mathaeus? Bihan, forget that damned eye. It suits you."

Bihan's chest erupted in a guttural roar. He drove the dagger point into the stone floor, muscles trembling, temple pounding. "Remove it, Shadi, or I'll—"

Shadi raised a hand, firm as a stay against a storm. "All right," he said, stepping forwards, closing the gap. "I will. But first, you need to hear why it's the worst idea you've ever had." His gaze flicked to the window's shifting light.

Bihan drew a ragged breath and gave a single nod.

"That marble—the eye of Montero—it changed colour because of the teleportation spell that trapped Syrek. Only a spell of that magnitude could've—"

"I know," Bihan cut across him. He scuffed his sandal on the flagstones, smoothing the pleats of his kilt. "The dreams I spoke of... I understand."

Shadi's stare sharpened. "Then you must see: if I take it from you, it will return to its master. To Montero. Do you understand what that means?"

Rabia, tracing the chipped paint on her nails, let pale crescents scar her fingertips. "Just say it plain," she muttered.

"The High Mage hasn't left Seaborne," Shadi pressed, his voice weighted with urgency. "He won't leave this place until he gets what he wants. If he reclaims that eye, it'll only amplify his standing. With it, he could bind the wyverns in a breath. Or force Rabia to unlock the stele's secrets."

"Or both." Bihan's chest tightened. "Just as he forced Syrek's teleportation. Translate the stele, command the wyverns, and Toussaint crowns himself Imperator of a reborn Imperium. Al-Qiyamah." His fingers hovered at the marble; it trembled beneath his touch. "Montero's status as Vizier will be restored. Not merely patriarch of a city, nor puppet to its princes, but the right hand of the Imperator."

Bihan mapped alliances and threats, but Montero's grand design at Toussaint's side remained a storm beyond his reach. Camila's treachery might've shredded her ties to Toussaint, but Montero's volatile reaction to the news convinced Bihan that his allegiance was as unbreakable as it was terrifying. His schemes left scars deeper than any blade.

"Fine," Bihan spat. "It needs a vessel. I understand. But why me? Can't another bear it?" Heat seared his lungs as the orb hummed, eager. "I *can't* harbour a fragment of him."

Shadi set a slender hand on his shoulder. "It's no longer him. It's relic, not master. A source, like my wand."

"And if Montero invokes that spell again? I could die."

Shadi's smile was crooked, wry. "Only if the bearer permits it to be cast, or the parchment-holder reads it aloud. The laws were written after Syrek's fall. Even Montero must obey."

Sir Mathaeus inclined his head, solemn. "Rules bind us all, even Mystics."

"More or less," Shadi murmured, grin flickering like a secret flame.

Bihan felt the weight of what went unsaid, but he trusted Shadi. If harm was meant, it would've come already.

Then screams tore through the corridor above. Commands bellowed, urgent and brutal. Bells in the Sail Ale's tower clanged in rapid succession, the clamour spilling through Seaborne like wildfire on dry hills. Steel rang as Bihan and Mathaeus drew their blades. Rabia's fingers brushed the ringed scabbards of her tomahawks. From the tunnels' black throat, the rattle of armour rose. The jailers came, lanterns swaying, boots thundering, closing in on the cells where the four had lingered too long.

The city was awake.

Bihan drove his splintered dagger through the first jailer's legs, the man collapsing with a cry that drowned beneath the clash of steel. A single thought pierced the chaos—yes, they now knew the stele's resting place, but where was the vault that housed both treasure and the subterranean Syrek?

Mathaeus' blade swept through the second jailer, the one who'd let them past only moments before. He wiped the edge clean on the fallen man's cloak as the body slid down, fingers streaked with cyan paint. Against the crimson pooling beneath him, the blue looked almost luminous. A clue. The carrack. The model ship hadn't been just idle craft.

Bihan stepped into the raw glare of the rising sun, holding the miniature ship aloft. Light bled through the sails until they blurred into ghostly blue. Squinting, he could barely discern the inked letters. Holding it at arm's length, he made out only the scrawling first word.

Shadi, his lower arm crudely bandaged in a jailer's torn cloak, took the model from him. His bony finger traced the ink with reverence. "'Bring the khorvo to Captain Contreras' vault beneath our king's landed ship,'" he read aloud. His voice faltered at the absence of detail. "No numbers. No map. Nothing to follow but shadows."

Bihan jerked his chin towards the crooked lanes he and Mathaeus had threaded. "We don't need a map. Look there—the bowsprit of that man-o'-war, looming over the city like a spear. That's where we go. In fast, out faster. Same as when Rabia and I gutted Sakogiannis' vaults."

Rabia gave a humourless chuckle. "Fast in, long out."

"Halt," Sir Mathaeus ordered, sheathing his sword with a click. He tilted his head, listening, his body taut. From the left alley drifted curses, muttered and venomous. The right lay silent, waiting.

Always the right, Bihan thought.

Before they moved, Mathaeus' words cut the air. "I'm no thief. I won't follow you to that ship. You three go on. I'll hold them off and meet you at the harbour. You won't find me. I'll find you. Now go."

They fled down the right-hand alley. Behind them rang the brutal music of steel: swords clashing, a ragged chorus of pain. Bihan risked a glance back. In the fog-lit gloom, Mathaeus' glowing blade cleaved a corsair's cutlass—and arm—in one devastating arc. The same killing stroke Bihan had once delivered to a garnok. His chest clenched. He missed his khopesh. He missed his left hand.

Corsairs combed the streets, fog shrouding their desperation. They overturned crates, ripped linens from lines, snarled at one another like dogs. A lone feral cat hissed, and they scattered. Had they read the tales of Bihan the Beauty, however, they would've known what a cat's hiss foretold.

At the alley's end they gathered beneath the shadow of the man-o'-war's massive bowsprit. Fog clung low, wrapping littered stones. Beyond stretched the polished avenues, swept bare for the king's gaze while refuse and rot were driven into alleys. Out of sight, out of mind. Fugitives belonged here.

By a smouldering barrel, Bihan pressed them against the rusted fence that circled the hilltop cemetery. He tapped the weakest section—an exit should they need it. Fog gave cover, but the sun would betray them soon enough. What he longed for more than concealment, however, was vengeance.

The marble in his socket thrummed so fiercely it churned his stomach. He cursed its pulse, then remembered how it had convulsed most violently when Montero drew near. Steadying his spinning head in both hands, he let a thin smile curl his lips. The eye would lead them to the vault. To Syrek. To Montero. His curse was his compass.

Boots clopped against stone. A splash echoed through a puddle. Two corsairs sauntered into view, swinging cutlasses and whistling a tune far too jaunty for the hour.

"Heard about the High Mage?" one muttered.

"Yeah," the other replied. "Scorched Captain Contreras' arm while she slept. Something to do with a tattoo... or a brand."

"Mm. Odd lot, that crew. Even before Camila killed ol' What's-His-Face and took command. Montero's furious. Said she no longer deserved the mark. Whatever that means. Never seen more loyal curs, though."

Their chatter slid towards mutiny until a corpulent corsair shouldered his way into the lane. He filled the gap, overturning crates with fat hands. Rabia moved like smoke, leading Shadi through the bars Bihan had kicked loose. They slipped into the cemetery, crouching beneath a monument carved as the Grim Reaper himself.

Bihan pressed against the chill stone, lungs full of salt-wet air. A grin, rare and sharp, bared his teeth. He remembered Fregor—the man who died so Montero and Camila Callo could drag them into this city. Fregor would've liked Seaborne.

They waited until nightfall, slipping from shadow to shadow, careful to avoid the reeling drunkards still prowling in hope of returning the escapees to Captain Contreras. From their high vantage, Bihan stole a glance back towards the Sail Ale. Somewhere in that maze of alleys, Sir Mathaeus still fought or hid. The paladin's honour was ironclad, but Bihan doubted he'd strike down a sodden fool too drunk to know whether he was kissing a bottle or a woman.

At last, they reached the city's crowning landmark: the landed ship. Bihan lingered beneath the twin moons' cold glow. Mana-lamps and neolyt glimmered like scattered jewels, but Seaborne itself lay in nature's cradle—walls dressed in ivy, gulls crying from their nests, vines curling along weather-worn balconies. Stone and timber breathed with green life. For an instant, Bihan stood still, taking it in as though imprinting his final sight of it. Far below, in the vault's depths, waited the gothic city that haunted him.

He could no longer feel the phantom tingling that once ran through his fingertips and toes, yet Bihan remembered it—how that surge had coursed through him when Rabia chose this path. The memory was as vivid as terror, as heady as salt wind.

Without thought, his hand found her forearm. Her warmth steadied him against the cold, tethering him more securely than steel. This time, she didn't pull away. Neither of them did. The silence between them lengthened, filled only by Shadi's impatient muttering as he studied the mountain-side doors. Bihan and Rabia held one another's gaze, each recognising the peril ahead, and the bond that bound them to it.

He drew a breath, the words of caution lingering on his tongue, but she cut him off with that familiar, knowing smirk. For a heartbeat, his gaze lingered on her in the moonlight, and he noticed anew the peculiar beauty he'd somehow overlooked: the generous swell of her chest beneath the rich folds of her clothing, the stark purity of her black lips, unexpectedly captivating against the brown curve of her jaw. A fleeting, impossible thought brushed his mind: how she might feel pressed against him, how her warmth might mingle with his own... but the sensation of fear sharpened it instantly. He realised why he thought such things: it was not desire, but the raw ache of loss. He wanted to remember every detail of her—her scent, the brush of her hair, the exact curve of her horns—so that no darkness, no distance, could ever take her from him.

A silent vow settled in his chest, stronger than any blade. They were friends, companions forged in fire, bound by a trust deeper than words. And yet, in some hidden corner of his heart, he knew he would love her always, wholly and irrevocably, as one loves a kindred spirit whose absence would leave the world hollow.

With that understanding anchoring him, he let the thought pass, and together they stepped forwards into the unknown.

XIV

The Sunless City

The ornate door beneath the landed ship's mountain pedestal wasn't hard to find. Bedecked in silver filigree and crowned with a gilded handle, it thrummed like a living thing as Bihan's false eye vibrated, hummed, even sparked beneath the moonlight. Ten identical doorways, carved from black stone, lined the weathered mountainside—each a promise of secrets within or below—but only one stirred to his marble's pulse.

The others stood dead and cold, their silence more menacing than indifference.

Rabia's spine stiffened, a twinge pulling at her body, and though she masked the wince, Bihan caught it. His gaze lingered, the questions unspoken: why had she sheathed her tomahawks for so long, withdrawn from the fight when battle had once been her breath? He feared he'd never learn the truth. Yet he recognised the shadows at work in her now. Returning to Syrek was no idle venture—it tore at her as sharply as the moment she'd enlisted beneath General Freja Torbjörn's banner. Then, her idol's standard had rallied them into a war that scattered comrades across the lands, forging scars deeper than any blade; and now, that same idol's corpse summoned them back to the hellscape.

Moving with deliberate caution, Bihan pressed his broad frame against the first door. Nothing. He tested the second, then the third, each one swallowing his presence in perfect silence. The marble eye in his skull grew restless, sparking against bone, but gave no answer until he returned to the door crowned in silver. At once the compulsion surged, the hum rattling his jaw and temple. He backed away, circled to test another, then returned again. Always the same. Always this door. At its centre the filigree caught the moonlight, dancing like veins of quicksilver, but when he reached for the gilt handle, his hand closed on solid stone.

"No handle at all," he muttered.

Rabia touched her lips, studying the design. "A trick."

Shadi rummaged through a battered corsair crate and drew out a length of rigging rope, three iron hooks tied along its length. He tossed it to Rabia. She dropped to one knee before the door, tracing the silver filigree until her fingers found a faint indentation—runes worn shallow with age. A mechanism. Sliding a hook into the topmost groove, she gave a sharp, decisive tug, and the door shuddered, a low vibration rolling through the stone like a creature roused from sleep.

Bihan drove the broken blade of his father into the hairline seam, the marble eye throbbing in rhythm with the door's awakening. As the runes flared with silver light, Rabia caught the rope taut, braced her arms, and heaved. The slab ground inwards on ancient tracks, reluctant but yielding. She didn't wait for the gap to widen. With the rope in hand, she surged through, movements coiled with raw purpose, and in that instant she seemed changed—reborn by the act itself, unafraid and sharpened by whatever waited in the vault's depths.

Bihan dropped into a crouch just inside the threshold, the marble's pulse warning of unseen snares. "Traps," he hissed, the word tearing out like a whip crack. "Rabia, wait!"

She only snorted, pressing forwards.

Her slipper settled on a perfect sandstone tile. A hollow click echoed beneath her weight. Bihan lunged, sweeping her legs out and dragging both her and Shadi down to the chill floor as marble statuettes lining the wall spat volleys of bolts. Arrows screamed across the chamber, sparking against the far masonry before a second barrage arced back, some dripping with a viscous green poison, others cloaked in tongues of fire.

Flattening his body across theirs, Bihan held them down, his words low and even. "Stay close. Mirror me."

Through the gloom, he mapped the vault's perils: pendulums suspended from alcoves, crescent blades glinting as they swayed on thick chains; a yawning pit whose rim gleamed with oily metal; and beyond that, the promise of treasure, hoard glittering in the shadows. His skull buzzed with the marble's dark song, whispering danger and delight in equal measure, but the flicker of worry in Rabia's face smothered his thrill like wind on flame.

He rolled free, slithering on his belly across the sandstone, hands sweeping for uneven slabs and hidden triggers. His fingers closed around fallen arrows scattered on the floor, their barbed shafts heavier than he expected, and he gathered them into his palm. Shadi shadowed him, pressing his hands flat to feel for disturbances in the stone, while Rabia crawled after, stubby arms tense but her breathing measured.

At the pendulums, Bihan paused. He fitted the sturdiest salvaged arrow into a chain-link with a deft flick. The blade shuddered, then swung free in a wide arc, cleaving through brittle bones littered across the passage floor—remnants of seekers less cautious than they. The sickening snap of splintering ivory carried through the chamber, and the pendulum's roar swelled and fell, each swing slower than the last until they hung motionless, quivering like sentinels poised to strike again. Up close, the iron etchings gleamed, spirals echoing those carved into Rabia's tomahawks. Bihan slipped past, nose wrinkling at a stinging tang not of steel but of stranger alloys, pungent and acrid.

When the path cleared, he beckoned the others forwards, leading them into the vault's deeper shadows. The sandstone gave way to crude, dark brick streaked with a venomous sheen. Shattered shards of stained glass, slick and green as bile, lay strewn across the ground beside the lip of a pit. They paused there, breaths unsteady, the silence pressing against them like a weight.

They'd reached the vault's heart.

Bihan crept to its edge. The pit stretched wide and black, no bottom visible—until a flicker revealed not shadows but a writhing carpet of scorpions, their pincers clacking in ceaseless hunger. No clear path spanned the chasm.

Shadi edged forwards, excitement lighting his features, eyes reflecting the pit's sinister gleam. He knelt beside a skeleton clinging to the pit's rim with only two crooked twigs wedged beneath its arms. The thing seemed frozen mid-struggle, jaw unhinged in a rictus grin. As Shadi's fingers brushed the gnarled wood, memory welled up inside Bihan—images of the sorceress' garden, the way Shadi's grandfather's staff had stirred air and soil, coaxing vines and blossoms into impossible life.

"This is illusion magic. It hides what's real. Remember my mother's garden?"

"Yes," Rabia answered, her boot scuffing hard against the slick black bricks. She tilted her horns towards the pit. "So, what do we do?"

"Dispel it," Shadi said simply.

He jostled the twigs, and the skeleton toppled, rattling into the abyss. For a breathless moment nothing happened, only the echo of bones striking unseen depths. Then, slowly, a stone walkway shimmered into being—broad slabs suspended above the writhing carpet of scorpions. Dust then poured down in choking clouds as chunks of mortar sheared from the ceiling, and the green glass beneath them fractured with wicked cracks.

"Across the walkway—now!" Bihan snarled, jabbing his dagger towards the conjured path.

They sprinted one by one, soles slipping on the new-formed stone, hearts hammering with each desperate step. Behind them the ceiling collapsed in a furious cascade of bricks and shards, a rockfall that sealed their retreat and plunged the vault into suffocating dark.

And then, through the haze of falling dust, a light bloomed. A pale, perfect glow that danced along the walls like moonfire, requiring no flame to breathe. It beckoned them.

The chamber ahead was littered with half-opened chests, their lids wrenched back as if pried by greedy hands and left agape to mock new intruders. Jewels lay spilt in heaps: rubies swollen as hearts, emeralds and sapphires cascading from overturned goblets, silver vases chased with the coils of sea serpents, and coins scattered across the stone like so many captive stars. At the chamber's centre burnt a lone torch, its wavering flame casting sparks across the glittering hoard.

But it was not the wealth that held their eyes—it was the lake of molten metal surrounding it, mercury glimmering in a restless, pallid mirror, hissing whenever green glass or glowing rubble spat into its surface.

"Liquid mercury," Rabia murmured, her tone flat and grim. "Don't let it touch your skin."

Picking their way across the unstable ground, they used chunks of collapsed masonry as stepping stones, each slab shifting beneath their feet as though trying to roll them into the shimmering death below. Still, they pressed on, inch by inch, until finally the torch and treasure lay within reach. Shadi collapsed onto his knees, chest heaving, hands trembling as he scooped fistfuls of gems into his palms. His eyes gleamed wide as a child's.

"I've never seen so much... never in my life."

"Yeah, yeah," Rabia snapped, brushing past him with a derisive snort. Her gaze had already fixed beyond the pile, searching for a truer prize. "Pretty baubles, deep challises, but there's our way forwards."

Bihan lifted a hand, stalling her impatience. He stole a glance at Shadi, whose vest was dusted in a faint golden sheen, and Rabia, whose horns glinted sharply in the torchlight as she tossed her head in annoyance. Treasure was nothing to either of them—they'd lived, bled, and lost too much for a chest of coins to sway their hearts. But for Shadi, the wonder was still unbroken, still innocent. It struck Bihan then, how fragile and rich that innocence was, more valuable than any gem.

"Hold on," he said softly.

Rabia huffed and spun. "I won't. Come on, Shadi. Stele in hand, I'll drown you in gold if you like. Let's move."

Bihan chuckled under his breath, nudging the magus upright with one shoulder. "Impatient and stubborn—that's our Rabia. Come on, Shadi, before she starts swinging."

Together they pressed beyond the treasure. The chamber narrowed into a fissure reeking of rot, a stench that clawed the throat like flesh left to bake in stagnant sun. Ragged howls drifted up from below, long and broken, promising only hunger and torment. Shadi paled; Rabia's eyes hardened to flint. Bihan felt his chest tighten, his pulse drum heavy in his skull. He could see their fear as plainly as his own, yet nothing could turn them back.

His fingers closed tighter around his father's fractured blade. Thoughts of betrayal wormed into his mind, and sweat cooled on his brow despite the suffocating heat. The hilt turned slick in his grip. Shadi caught his eye, and in that instant the magus' trembling smile and violet gaze burnt away the shadows gnawing at him.

"How deep is this chasm?" Rabia crouched at the fissure's lip, peering into the endless black.

Bihan kicked a loose stone. They waited as it tumbled for long, echoing heartbeats until a faint click whispered back. No light, no guide. Just the void answering their question.

Shadi shifted uneasily. "Didn't tell us much. Landed on... something solid, maybe."

"Torch," Bihan muttered, still staring into the abyss. "Fetch it."

Shadi hurried back, retrieving the central flame. Rabia meanwhile looped her frayed rope around a crumbling, oil-slicked column and trimmed the excess with her tomahawk. The cut was clean, deliberate, and Bihan wondered again why she measured so carefully.

He dropped the torch into the dark. Its fall revealed pillars of black stone, polished like obsidian yet veined with oil that glistened as it caught the flame. Each was carved with jagged hieroglyphs that sparked faint arcs of electricity, crackling as the torch passed. For a moment the fire sputtered, dying and rekindling in rapid stutters, before finally striking bottom. A dull thud, not a splash. Stone, not water.

Bihan exhaled through his teeth. "Deeper than we dared guess, but the rope'll hold. Slack's close—we'll only sprain an ankle at worst."

Shadi's pearwood wand traced the carvings on the nearest column, violet eyes wide with awe. "These were in Freja's memories," he whispered. "Not as we saw in the globe, Bihan, but this is it. This is Syrek."

Bihan's throat constricted around the name. "Syrek... buried beneath Seaborne. Who would've thought?" His voice rasped low, heavy with both dread and wonder. "After everything, we've come back to its ruin."

A rumble shuddered through the ground, and pebbles rattled loose from the ceiling to skitter down the carved columns. Bihan's thoughts leapt at once to the Enkharan wyrms: obscenely long, subterranean titans whose oily spittle fuelled the desert pumpjacks. The gleam coating these pillars had the same slick sheen, but the hieroglyphs etched into them were not natural. Fresh gouges, purposeful hands. Worshippers had marked these stones, and worship always meant danger.

His fingers strayed to the jagged hilt of his father's broken blade. Rabia tossed the end of the frayed rope over the ledge and tightened the knot around the crumbling column with steady hands, while Shadi stood beside her, offering a small nod meant more for himself than the others. They were ready—or as ready as anyone could be—to descend into Syrek's buried heart.

"That day at Belmont Bank," Bihan said, his timbre carrying across the slick stone, "did you ever imagine I'd lead us back here, Rabia? Back to Syrek."

"Not for a second," she admitted, massaging her shoulder where his earlier tackle had left a bruise. Her laugh was dry, though not unkind. "I thought we'd storm some banditos, snatch the damsel, and vanish into the night. Turns out fate had higher stakes for a pair of honour-bound fools."

At the crevice, Shadi hovered with his parchment half-unfurled, breath rising sharp and shallow. Sweat traced his temple. His violet eyes flicked to Bihan's, and for a moment both held steady. Then, with quiet resignation, Shadi tucked the parchment back into his vest and let the spell fade unspoken. He offered the faintest of smiles. Bihan's answering curve of lip was fleeting, almost reluctant.

"Look," Rabia murmured, tilting her horns towards the shadows below. Across the far wall, the faint glow of torchlight revealed an iron-banded door. She reached towards its shape, tracing the lock in the air with a finger. "Recognise that?"

Bihan slipped Rabia's polished tomahawks free from their loops. Their blades caught the light, gleaming like crescent moons, and when he held them against the outline of the lock, the fit was unmistakable. His smirk was razor-edged.

"Stolen from a prince so fair he might've sung his vanity in taverns instead of marching to war," he said. "These were his showpieces, not war-steel. Tailored to his pride."

Rabia's lips bent into a grim, knowing curve. "Then we fit them where they belong."

"We must," Bihan answered, resting a hand on her shoulder with a weight that was both steady and pleading. "That stele can't fall to anyone—whether they're capable of reading it or not. Not to Montero's might or Callo's guile. It would crown a tyrant. A tyrant who'd chain freedom, ignite wars, and herald Muam Al-Dyn. The End of Days. We've come too far, bled too much, to let it happen."

Shadi drew himself tall, the boyish awe gone from his face, replaced with a pale but genuine resolve. "I'm with you," he said simply.

And Rabia—Rabia, who had lately worn more scowls than smiles—let warmth breach the shadow beneath her horns. "Always," she promised.

Bihan's grip tightened on his father's broken sword, the weapon's jagged edge catching the torchlight from below.

Beneath them, firelight trembled against iron. Before them, destiny waited.

XV

The Stillness of Stone and Oil

Bihan didn't hesitate. He seized the rope and descended, the fibres rough against his palms, fragrant with the earthy tang of turnips and cabbage. The smell vanished as the necropolis swallowed him whole. A pall of darkness closed around his shoulders, dense enough to smother breath itself. No hum of insects. No scrape of stone. No taste but dust on the tongue. Rabia followed at once, Shadi after her, all three careful to steer wide of the towering pillars that loomed like sentinels.

Sandals and boots struck stone rimed with damp. The chill seeped through leather into bone. Bihan tested the anchor, tugging hard, then secured the rope about the ribs of a corpse still skewered on an ancient spear. Only then did the whispers come—skittering and chittering in the unseen corners. A rush, as though the chamber's last breath had fled and left them at the lip of the Eternal Abyss.

A sudden spark burst from his false eye. Flame and current seared his lashes and stubble; the pain needled through his skull. He pressed a palm to the socket, a groan in his throat. When he drew his hand away, light streamed forth: a fuchsia brilliance, sharp as a beacon. It cut across the cavern, glancing off the pillars' oil-slick sheen. The sight rooted him to the spot. He knew this place. Too well.

The scream of war echoed in his head—men torn apart, fire rolling. His jaw locked, shoulders bracing for a fight long ended. Then Rabia's hand closed over his, firm and steady, bones creaking under her strength. The tether of her grip wrenched him back from the pit of memory. He exhaled, forcing himself into the present.

"Bihan." Shadi crouched low, wand twisting between his fingers like wrung cloth. At his knees lay three husks of skin and tattered garments, limp as deflated wineskins.

Bihan joined him, lowering into the glow of his strange light. He knew them instantly—the *Delphine's* captain, the merchant of barrels, and Felipe Contreras. His throat tightened to stone. "Your theory?" he asked.

Shadi flicked his wand and conjured a trembling sphere. Within its shimmer unfolded their path: Montero shadowing them from the outset, each step nudged and guided by his hand and by the captain who once stood proud at his side. The vision darkened to the slit of throats, the neat peeling of flesh in curling ribbons, the grafting of skin into robes that flexed like living muscle with necromancy. Costumes.

Shadi turned his face away, lips drained of colour.

Rabia didn't. Her gaze stayed fixed, eyes like chiselled flint. "We were meant to come here. Who else could read the stele? Who else can command armies by name alone but the Last Barbarian, Hero of the Syrek War?" Her tone carried neither awe nor fear—only resolve. "Camila wrapped herself in these tales until they became armour. She dreamt of a lord's seat, and now, after betraying Montero and abandoning Toussaint's cause, she claws for a throne over a rotting land."

Shadi's voice was a thin reed. "She never counted on me. My magic was never written into her design." His eyes sought Bihan's.

"Whether by fate or plot," Bihan said, rising and striding towards the tomahawk-marked door, "we go forwards. We take the stele. Then we leave."

Rabia's stance hardened, arms folding across her chest, tomahawks flashing at her hips. "And after? Do we drift like Freja? Nomads without aim? My oath binds me to the wyverns, but I won't bind you both to the same chain."

"I've a better way." The light of his false eye washed the lock, its fuchsia glow meeting the hum of runes etched deep into stone. "We read the stele. We find the wyverns and warn them—tell them to flee, to follow the path of the few surviving dragons who vanished after their revolt. Then we destroy the stele and bury what remains. Lost to time."

Shadi inclined his head, but Rabia's brow furrowed.

"Too simple," she murmured, stepping closer. "Why didn't Freja think of that?"

Silence welled. Bihan's mouth opened, but Shadi's words filled the gap. "Freja broke after the war—before she wandered the wastes. Her mind rotted with grief. She wasn't thinking clearly."

Rabia's lips twisted into a half-sneer, half-sorrow. "At least she carried guilt." She unhooked her tomahawks and set them into Bihan's hands. "Take them. Use them."

The weapons slid into the locks with a perfect fit. Metal clicked, then ground. The door moaned against its hinges—yet when the noise faded, nothing stirred. Bihan's hand twitched towards his old key before he remembered where he'd left it. His fingers brushed the false eye instead, an itch burning beneath the marble.

The tomahawks fractured with a shriek, shards tumbling to Rabia's slippers. Her sharp intake of breath cut the silence. The door didn't yield. She kicked it once, twice, then again, the opulent slippers striking stone as curses hissed through her teeth. At last, a dull boom answered from within. Slowly, ponderously, the door began to swing.

Pale green lamps ignited in sequence along the archway, drowning his fuchsia light in hiss and steam. Bones lined the threshold—skeletal lords draped in jewelled robes, wealth enough to ransom a kingdom strewn across their remains. Bihan stepped over them, the glow from his false eye throwing stark shadows. Every flicker sent knives through his lashes, memories clawing of his parents' end.

Across from him, Shadi averted his gaze, a sheen of moisture gathering on his brow.

"A dead end," Rabia spat.

But before them loomed four esoteric doors, each bearing a grotesque lock shaped in mimicry of the oily pillars. Bihan's chest tightened. This was the chamber from his dream. These were the doors he'd walked through in shadow.

"We could split up," Shadi whispered, words brittle.

"No." Bihan's refusal cracked like stone. He rubbed the socket of his false eye, the itch now a constant flame. "We stay together. And no one touches those doors."

He traced the circle inscribed in the floor, following the wizard's path from dream-memory. Folding his legs, he lowered himself cross-legged into the centre, eyes closed, palms open to the void. The oil-black columns and green fire bled together at the edges of vision.

"Bihan!" Rabia's tone whipped across the chamber. "Stand. Do you hear me?"

"Trust me," he murmured, steady as rock. "Sit within the circle."

She wavered, then obeyed, folding herself with reluctant grace, legs taut, hands open. Shadi slithered into place beside them, wand tucked away, a trembling hand dragging across his damp brow.

"This is folly," he muttered. "Meditating in a necropolis."

"Then don't," Bihan said, quiet as the earth's pulse.

The floor then quaked beneath them, and the room was gone. The circle dissolved, and in its place rose a hall so vast it seemed to swallow even palaces whole. Columns of blackened stone marched in endless ranks, each crowned with a brazier that spat emerald flame. Hooded figures—gaunt, towering, robed in fabric that writhed like smoke—lined the path in silent procession. They stood as priests might, guardians of some forbidden rite. Bihan recognised them at once. They were the same apparitions that stalked through his nightmare.

At the far end, a staircase soared towards a colossal statue carved from slick black stone. A skull-face stared down at them, its eye sockets worn smooth by centuries, hollow and hungry. From the statue's ribcage jutted a dagger, gleaming like bone polished by ritual use—identical to the weapons clutched by the hooded figures in that same nightmare.

"My... I've seen this," Shadi stammered, breath shallow. "Through Freja's eyes."

Bihan's chest constricted. The war-screams he'd buried howled to life, clamouring in the green-lit gloom.

Runes crawled across the statue's pedestal: letters jagged and foreign, but their dread bled through even without meaning. Bihan's throat tightened against the urge to turn and flee. Then Rabia's hand found his, warm and grounding, her presence an anchor in the green gloom. They stood together—three against the necropolis' ancient will.

Shadi placed one tentative foot on the first step. The stone cracked beneath his weight but held. Black oil welled from the columns, seeping like tears. It streamed down the hall in rivulets and pooled at the base of bas-reliefs carved into the wall they came through: war-scenes etched in uncanny motion, warriors writhing, blades flashing, faces in eternal screams.

"Now my turn," Shadi whispered, climbing another step. "Freja saw the stele here—at the statue's feet."

"It's oil and stone," Bihan muttered, flat with disappointment.

"No," Rabia said, firm as a command. "You're not looking hard enough."

She strode past them, fearless. As she neared the statue's knee, every apparition along the dais swivelled in perfect unison, empty hoods locking on her. Bihan's fingers twitched towards his hilt. His false eye itched. He never forgot the phantom tingle that'd once warned him.

Rabia raised a trembling hand and pressed it into the slaggy oil coating the statue. A spark leapt from stone to skin—searing her nails and fingertips. She clenched her jaw, muscles knotting at her shoulders, but didn't draw back. With a hiss through her teeth, she bit down on her lip until blood welled, then plunged both hands into the slick black liquid.

Lightning raced up her arms in cruel spirals, outlining her in a halo of pain. The stench of scorched flesh hissed against the chamber's low, resonant drone. Beneath the slick surface, something massive stirred. Slowly, drawn forth by a force older than speech, the basalt stele revealed itself, rising like a leviathan from the deep.

Rabia screamed—a raw, ragged cry torn from her chest. Shadi recoiled, wand half-raised, while Bihan lunged to her side. His good hand grasped the old basalt, sinews straining until fire scorched his shoulders. Together they wrenched it free. With a wet sucking sound, the stele slipped from the oil's embrace, toppling into Rabia's arms. She staggered, knees buckling, and Bihan caught her as they both collapsed.

The apparitions drifted nearer. Their robes whispered across the steps, arms unfolding as if in prayer—or in readiness to embrace the living.

"Up!" Shadi hissed, dropping to help. He hauled Bihan to his feet, but Rabia shoved him aside. Still clutching the relic, she dragged it step by step down the dais. Pain carved lines across her face, yet her grip never faltered. When at last she cleared the statue's shadow, she let the stele fall in the centre of the chamber, surrounded on all sides by the silent congregation.

"This... this is it," she whispered, pointing to the Megaran script etched deep into the basalt.

Bihan's marble eye burnt brighter as he leant in. "A masterful copy of your people's stelae," he murmured, fingertip tracing the worn lines. "Remarkable."

"See those chips?" Shadi produced his parchment with a shaking hand. "Marks from her exile."

Rabia guided Bihan's gaze, lifting his chin until his strange light fell across the words. Her own scorched finger followed the script as she began to translate, her voice low, syllables rolling with cadence neither man dared repeat. The drone of the chamber thickened with every phrase, until the walls seemed to vibrate with her utterance.

She faltered near the end. Her lips quivered; fear cracked her composure. Shadi's parchment slipped from his grip, his hands trembling too fiercely to hold it.

"It speaks of the birth of a new race," she said, voice barely more than breath. "The wyverns." Her fingers fell from Bihan's chin.

Free from her hold, Bihan's lone eye snapped to Shadi, who stiffened, hiding the parchment beneath his boots.

Rabia pressed on, deliberate, composed despite the quiver in her jaw. "Freja's prose breathes with a skill no khorvo could ever master. We craft steel and gunpowder, but not words like these. She warns the reader—kin or kindred—that they must guard these creatures in secrecy. If they are to be moved, or visited, their current refuge is..."

Bihan's hand clamped over her mouth. "Our enemies may listen."

Rabia leant close, whispering against his palm, breath warm. "Seaborne's Cove, hidden deep in the mountains. They've slept under our noses all along."

The words turned his blood to fire. His marble eye flared, spitting arcs of lightning across the stele. He whirled to Shadi, rooted in place, parchment concealed but trembling. The thrumming grew in his skull, fierce and insistent. It was never like this, not since—

An accent cleaved the silence. "All you had to do was finish that sentence."

Curly-toed boots, flamboyant and ostentatious, broke into the glow. From the gloom materialised the High Mage himself. Montero. His Syreki robes gleamed with pristine silk, a mockery of priestly splendour, tailored sharp to a body that carried treachery in its bones. Abandoning his Aledhyn attire, he'd become the traitorous and conniving vizier once more—pointy nose, manicured beard and all.

Bihan staggered back. A lightning-shaped scar raked across Montero's left cheek, burning with the same fuchsia glow as the marble's iris. Memory crashed down—of the ritual that tore Syrek into the wyrms' domain, lightning melting flesh from bone, and tearing eye from socket.

Montero's tattooed fingers drifted to the scar, tracing its trough with almost tender familiarity. They lingered on the cratered pockmarks that marred his face. His lips curled.

"Plague of Aledhyn," he said softly. "Hideous, yes. But not contagious—not to the people of our Realm."

"Plague scars, eh?" Shadi glanced at the parchment beneath his boots. "You're far older than you claimed when meeting my mother."

"Shadimtha Coelho." Montero's bow was mock-gentle, oily as his voice. "Magus, not sorcerer like your mother. A wise choice." His eyes narrowed. "Now hand me that parchment your whore mother stole."

Shadi planted his feet on either end of it and stepped forwards. In one twist, the parchment tore in two. Fragments fluttered about his ankles before dissolving into sparks, as though the spell itself gave a final sigh before vanishing into nothing. Whatever magic had been contained within that greasy, stained, and soft parchment... was gone.

Montero's roar split the air. His staff ignited in a pillar of crimson blaze. Shadi's wand flicked out from his sleeve, and a translucent shield blossomed to drink the flames, scattering them in showers of green motes. He countered at once, emerald fireflies swarming the chamber. Bihan's chest thundered with each strike and counter. He felt his trust in Shadi root itself like a blade driven deep.

Montero staggered back, shadow coiling around his weapon arm—vanishing, then reappearing a stride away, staff levelled at Bihan. "Give me my eye, barbarian," he hissed.

Bihan tapped it, letting the glow of the chamber glimmer across its surface. He drew his shoulders broad. "I think I'll keep it."

Montero's twitch began small, shoulders jerking as if his body belonged to another, or controlled by a puppeteer. A chuckle clawed out of his throat, warped into high, cracking laughter. The apparitions on the dais stirred as though roused by his madness, robes rasping in the silence.

"Three loyal friends!" he crowed, clapping sharply. Then he vomited a torrent of black blood, stinking of rot and plague. "Three buffoons! You, barbarian, did your loyal magus explain the eye? The spell on that parchment? No!" Each word spat like acid. "Do you want to know? He carried the *identical* spell I used to drag Syrek beneath the earth; the same that cost me my eye!" He licked blood from his cracked lips, eyes fever-bright. "His mother entrusted your precious Shadimtha with my rite, right down to the final syllable. Not because she believed in his destiny, but because she lusted for my triumph—minus the bloodshed of war, of course. She wanted Syrek, and *he* was going to deliver it to her without question."

Bihan turned his back with a grunt, jaw stone tight. Shadi's knuckles whitened on his wand. The gnat had already chosen, already torn the parchment. Already defied her design. Shadimtha Coelho was a victim. Nothing more.

"Khorvo!" Montero snapped at Rabia, voice cracking like a whip. "Translate it for me! Give me the wyverns, and I'll drown you in gold."

Rabia never lifted her head from the stele. Her fingers traced the lines of her ancestors. "Bugger yourself sideways, madman." Her voice was cool as steel.

The chamber hushed. Even breath seemed unwelcome. A fissure groaned through the ceiling, and green fire guttered along the braziers. Chunks of dust rained down. The painterly patriarch above, father of the Tomahawk Prince, was split from his sons. Bihan shifted his weight, eye fixed on Montero.

"What riches, *wizard*? What'll be left to buy in your apocalypse? Piss off before I kill you."

Montero stroked his salt-and-pepper beard with trembling fingers, voice softening into a desperate plea. "Then only speak the location. On my honour, I'll leave." His glowing eye flickered.

"You've no honour," Shadi spat, stepping close, wand raised. "You're desperate, clawing for a legacy. You stitch grand titles to your name—wizard, high mage, vizier—so history won't forget you. But it's emptier than your soul."

"Careful, boy..." Montero's grin widened. "You don't know the power of my *aard*."

"There is no *aard*, you pompous cock," Shadi snapped. "Only magic—pure, relentless, and free. You didn't birth it, and you'll never own it."

The floor rolled like a sea swell beneath them, the apparitions shifting as though weighing his words.

Montero slammed his staff to the ground, his voice a booming sermon. "Fools! That void you crossed on your descent was no fear-born illusion. It was the aether itself—a fracture in the world, a wellspring of raw *aard*, nature's own breath! Magic is a myth spun by the powerful, a divine fairy tale spun by liars to justify their meddling—to keep the masses shackled. But *aard*—unbound, living, fierce—will endure. When Toussaint claims the throne and Muam Al-Dyn rises, the false divines will betray you, your fragile spells will shatter, but *aard* will shield the people. And I, Grand Vizier of the Imperium, will wield it!"

"Like you protected Syrek, Vizier?" said Rabia.

His shoulders sagged. "Syrek was an experiment weakened by war. My nerves snapped. Lives were lost. I failed..." His fingers brushed his scar. "But I won't fail again. Muam Al-Dyn must rise. The world must start anew. And Al-Qiyamah is the first step. The wyverns are the first step."

Silence reclaimed the chamber, heavy as the stone around them. In another time, Bihan might've agreed. But that man was dead, and he would never return. Only the here and now remained.

With resolute fingers, he drew his father's fractured sword—the same blade Montero had once shattered as though it were kindling. The earth convulsed beneath their feet, each tremor rattling his ribs. Bihan fixed his gaze on the wizard's ravaged face, daring the smallest hope that Montero might recognise the weapon's pedigree. He did not. He didn't even glance at it.

The flagstones buckled and split.

An oblivious, or worse, a sympathetic, villain was the cruellest kind: too human, too familiar. That was why in Bihan's tales recounted for bards and scholars, villains had always been rendered flat, mere silhouettes on a stage—easier to slay, easier to forget. Pity was poison. Yet it rose now, unbidden, in his chest. He crushed it with an oath: Montero and Camila would fall, and vengeance would be fulfilled.

He lunged, dagger poised for the throat, but a surge of raw force hurled him back. His spine struck the statue's slick surface, oily currents searing into him as if the stone itself conspired against him. The world reeled in sickening circles before he collapsed onto the dais.

The apparitions were gone. Dissolved into heaps of ragged, black cloths. In their stead, the earth split wide, spewing dirt and sand into a ravenous maw. From the fissure clawed a creature of nightmare: eight-legged, grotesque, its swollen abdomen dragging across fractured flagstones. Bihan's breath caught. He remembered that rasping warning, spoken by the very thing that had stolen his eye—half a sense.

The manticore rose before them, glistening with wyrm-oil. Its guttural inhalation rattled the hall, forked tongue tasting the necropolis air. One eye burnt red; the other, a golden stone, throbbed with currents beyond any mortal technology, crackling as it had in desert wastes. A predatory grin like a wound split its jaws.

"Should chance or sorcery cross our paths again," it hissed, voice thick with cruel amusement, "I'll exact a toll beyond a token." At its side, staff in hand, Montero's lips curved in perfect echo of the beast's mirth. He no longer bargained. He understood the manticore's law, and with a gesture as swift as lightning, seized its allegiance. The monster bowed to his will, and the tables turned with terrible finality. "If ever I lay eyes on you again, only death will settle the debt."

XVI

The Weight of the Stele

Montero's hawk-like nose carved a cruel silhouette as he stretched to murmur perverse commands into the manticore's ear. His lips moved in fevered whispers, but the beast's gaze never strayed. Its leer—a grotesque contortion of fang and muscle—lingered on the three companions, twitching each time Montero drew back, only to deepen as he leant in again, sowing venom with every breath.

At last, the High Mage stepped away. Bihan raised his father's fractured sword like a desperate prayer, its weight trembling in his grip. Behind him, Rabia's eyes fastened to the basalt stele. She dragged it against her shins and crouched on its chill surface, guarding it with a ferocity that cut deeper than steel. At Bihan's flank stood Shadi, pearwood wand levelled though his knees shook. He held firm regardless, eyes alight with resolve.

The odds couldn't have been starker. This battle was un-winnable. Yet Shadi's fragile courage—clear and brittle as blown glass—blazed against despair. Bihan felt pride stir within him, sharp and bittersweet. Perhaps, through some unseen alchemy, his own tenacity had passed like a torch to the magus.

Montero, their tormentor, had shed terror for something far worse. Confidence returned to him like armour reforged: his chest swelled, his spine snapped straight as a lance, his chin lifted with practiced poise. Words tumbled out with the smoothness of an old orator, every syllable betraying the raw fear that'd shaken him only moments before. His grin spread wide, teeth bared in triumph, and the sight of it made Bihan's blood run colder than stone.

With the manticore crouched at his side, hope seeped from the chamber. Their choice was as brutal as it was simple: translate the stele or die beneath the beast's claws. Were the creature left to its own devices, their deaths would already have been written. Bihan's only prayer was that Montero's arrogance might still invite a bargain. If not, he'd no other plan.

That certainty sat in his belly like a lead weight. His charms had already been squandered on Camila—once adoring, now treacherous. All that remained was his father's broken sword. Paired with its lost khopesh, it had sung through arcs wide and deadly, but alone its reach was insultingly short. He feared the coming clash not because he doubted his will, but because he knew with fatal clarity: they would lose.

They would die. Nothing he might do now could alter that truth.

"I could boast for hours about my ingenuity, how I manoeuvred you here like game pieces on a board," Montero said, twisting his rich-fabric sleeve between his fingers. "But I won't waste breath. All you need remember is this: if you want something done, you do it yourself. Relying on pyrates who masquerade as gentrified corsairs is a mistake no one survives twice."

He drifted forwards, curly-toed boots skimming over discarded cloaks littering the broken flagstones. The manticore followed with ponderous menace, its bristled, arachnid legs splintering ancient stone at every step. The sound summoned Bihan's father's warnings to memory: grim lessons on such abominations. His eye flicked to his blade, and he remembered... To strike down a manticore, one must stand close enough to taste its foul breath, to feel the sting of venomous mist when steel pierced true.

Bihan's lips curved into a bitter smile. If they were doomed, then at the very least his blade would scar that wretched flesh, perhaps even shorten its monstrous years.

"I've spent years among arrogant magi, Montero," Bihan said, voice level, steady as a whetstone. "And watching you now, I see your vaunted *aard* is no different from their spells. The same pride, only swollen beyond measure."

"Don't lump me with their kind, barbarian!" Montero snapped, flinging his arms wide. A rippling surge of force burst from him, thundering down the hall. Shadi's pearwood wand lifted in a blur of silver light, a shield blossoming to drink the onslaught and cast it harmlessly into shadow. "Magi," Montero scoffed. "I only dissect their arts. I study by means your little brain can't fathom."

The manticore's golden eye pulsed with a mechanical hum that made the atmosphere vibrate. It lurched forwards, each hairy leg smashing stone like half-a-dozen iron hammers.

"Spare us your sermons on *aard* and aether," Bihan retorted, cutting his gaze towards Rabia. She'd edged closer behind him, fingers bone-white against the stele's edge. "You're nothing more than a tyrant who sows wars for sport and puppeteers beasts to prove your greatness. Or is it Captain Contreras who tugs your strings? Your chain of command seems... tangled."

"Enough." Montero slammed his staff down before the manticore's slavering maw. The beast halted in a convulsion of arcane force, its lip peeling back, legs twitching like misfired gears. "You thought you could stall, snatch my stele, and craft some noble tale of escape? This isn't one of your novellas."

Bihan lunged. Alihan's broken sword flashed, sweeping for Montero's ribs. The quarterstaff leapt to meet it, wood grinding steel with a thunderous screech, hurling the blade sideways. It slashed across the manticore's flank, carving shell. The beast shrieked, a hideous sound, and reeled back—only to whip forwards again, its aculeus plunging into cracked stone where Bihan had stood a heartbeat before.

Dagger in hand, Bihan twisted beneath a flurry of razor-sharp strikes. A violet bolt of energy slammed into his shoulder and threw him sprawling across the shattered flagstones, the impact scraping breath from his chest. He tasted iron and old dust. Shadi surged forwards, drawing a row of oversized sapphire skulls from the air; they hovered for a breath, jaws frozen mid-scream, then raced in a jagged wave of light at Montero and the manticore. Sulphur and the singed tang of burnt toast filled the cavern; the skulls made contact and the beast staggered, retreating on spidery legs that scraped stone like a dozen broken hammers.

Montero melted into shadow, a faint ember where his eye should be, and the hall shivered with the sound of spells. Bihan rolled under the beast's belly and slashed with Alihan's broken sword; the steel bit shallow grooves in chitin, blunted and sung, and the manticore answered with a rage that shook the bones of the necropolis. It drove its massive torso down as if it would crush the world, stone spalling like rain. Bihan rolled aside on hands slick with sweat and blood. The creature's hairy legs followed with tidal blows; age had dulled its grace but not its force. He slipped beneath the flurry between limbs, every movement carved out of pure, hot desperation.

Rabia stirred, a coiled presence at Shadi's side. Her fingers hovered near the rings of her tomahawk scabbards; in the blue-black light of incantations, her intent showed like a drawn blade. Bihan flipped, found purchase behind the beast and unleashed a string of curses that felt as much ritual as insult. The manticore lashed its segmented tail to skew him, but

Bihan met the strike with his dagger and drove it deep into the metasoma. The creature roared with a sound like splitting mountains and collapsed, its vast weight slamming Bihan's skull into the floor; stars bloomed, then a red veil took his sight.

Blind, pinned beneath the monster's rump, he stabbed at chitin, each thrust scraping uselessly. A low, satisfied chuckle rolled from the creature. Shadi vaulted, sliding his wand up his sleeve and clinging to the warm, bucking hide. He rode the manticore's spasms like a madman on a stallion and, when Bihan pitched Alihan's blade at him, Shadi caught the haft and tried to bisect the aculeus. An invisible force flared between blade and barb and flung the steel away before turning it to dust. The air, thick with the smell of burning timber and fresh rain, laced with cinnamon.

A protective ward was cast. Montero wouldn't lose his puppet so easily. The manticore bucked and cast Shadi from its back with a hiss, dragging the boy beside Bihan. Both lay prone on slick stone, the beast's weight caging them like a tomb.

"Clever," Montero said from the smoke-dark, stepping as if to inspect a fine instrument. He circled the trapped pair and then, with a ceremonial calm, seized Rabia by a horn. The staff's spearhead rested beneath her chin until the skin split, and a bead of blood surged like a dark pearl. He held her there, as if waiting for a reaction, eyes bright with cruel curiosity. "You knew the heart lies in its aculeus, Shadimtha. Impressive."

Rabia endured the pain, jaw set.

"Listen, you bug-eyed bitch," Montero hissed. "Translate the stele, or I'll command my pet to slaughter your friends."

The manticore shuddered through its massive frame. "I'm nobody's pet, Mystic. Don't make me your enemy."

Montero's hand flicked dismissively. "A jest," he said, lightness feigning control.

Rabia's mouth curved in a small, dangerous smile. There was a plan, quiet and lethal. "Before you kill us," she said, voice calm as stone, "would you not like your eye back?"

Montero paused. Laughter came, coarse and theatrical. "I'll pry it from his corpse. Who needs a source when you command such a *pet*?" Confidence sticky with certainty.

At that, the horror released its hold on Bihan and Shadi. It pivoted instead towards Montero, and the High Mage took a step towards the basalt stele—its ancient script poised on the brink of revelation. A translation by the khorvo at his mercy.

"I'll warn you again," the manticore rumbled, voice like grinding stone. "I'm nobody's pet."

"Silence!" Montero screeched. "You answer to me! You serve me, subterranean abomination!"

For a heartbeat the beast seemed to chafe beneath his command, then it lunged with arachnid speed. It vaulted over the stele and Rabia, smashing flagstone and throwing up a spray of grit. High Mage Montero stumbled backwards, scrambling towards the dais' colossal statue. One brush against its oily surface sent a bolt of crackling energy through his sleeves and flung his quarterstaff wide with a ping. He scrambled, the illusion of mastery slipping like a robe.

In the gap, Rabia snapped her fingers, eyes locked on the basalt stele. She signalled Bihan forwards. He hoisted the slab despite its weight; the salvaged ropes and hooks coiled at its flanks. He mustered the stele onto his shoulder like a harnessed burden, grit and judgement weighing against his neck. The apparitions, once scattered, now converged in a twisted circle, torn between the raging beast, the retreating wizard, and Bihan with the stele.

Shadi dove for the dagger's dusty remains, but Bihan yanked him back with a sureness that steadied the boy. He tried to pull Rabia to safety; she shrugged free and scrambled up the dais to stand at the manticore's flank, defiant and small against that vast, terrible anatomy.

"You're nobody's pet, great manticore," she intoned compellingly. "This one," she spat at Montero, "is unworthy of your loyalty. Just as that boy was unworthy of sacrifice."

The beast's pride flared; it straightened, throat pulsing like a drum. "I'll slay this *Mystic* first, then you, short one, then the rest."

The hall breathed around them, emerald flames guttering, and in the sudden hush the world felt its old axis tilt. Bihan set his shoulders beneath the stele and prepared to move. The plan was crude, immediate, absolute: get the stele out of there. Survive.

"This wretch deserves death, but not by your claws. Your glorious pelt must remain unstained," Rabia said, her tone unwavering. Shadi stooping to claim the quarterstaff that skittered at his feet, while the manticore crouched, all coiled muscle and patient hunger. "Raze this hall," she intoned, each syllable a bright shard. "Tear down beam and battlement. Send Montero to oblivion with his enemies, O great manticore, devourer of eyes and virgin's breath. Let the end be worthy of song. Bards will chant your name and honour the sacrifice that brought us all low."

A hiss threaded the cavern as the creature's tongue flicked like a wet blade. Its tension eased in a terrible slow surrender. "One death to still all voices," it rumbled. "I've lived long enough. Let me die. Let *us* die."

Rabia turned, a small, sombre smile shaping at the corner of her mouth; a smile that held the plan Bihan feared and honoured in equal measure. Dread iced his limbs as the apparitions, drawn like moths to flame, drifted towards the dais. They converged around Rabia, the manticore, and Montero's craven, pleading figure—a ring of shadowed witnesses.

"Bihan, what's happening?" Shadi's voice cracked.

He couldn't answer.

A familiar emptiness yanked him inwards—the memory of Fregor's burial clawed loose, throat closing on the taste of soil and salt. Invisible hands clamped at his lungs. He gasped through the panic, staring at Rabia as she spoke to the horror that would claim her life. The manticore inclined its massive head in slow, deliberate assent as Rabia's speech wove a tapestry of glory and the sacred grandeur of death. Yet Bihan heard none of her words, only saw a plea in those enormous, ever-dilated eyes he'd once mocked.

Through that silent gaze she asked one thing of her old companion: protect the wyverns and carry on her sacred mission. In turn, to honour her promise to Freja, Rabia would collapse Syrek's seat of oppression and drag its jailers into ruin, sparing only a single life for Bihan's retribution.

"Fitting, *Hero of Syrek*," she whispered, words lost amid the apparitions' susurrus. "That I die saving you, again."

Saving me, again?

The notion struck him with a confusion that made his thoughts stumble. Then the manticore reared, a mountain of segmented limbs blotting the vault in its shadow.

Its roar split the necropolis. A monstrous chitinous fist shattered the statue above the dais. Stone rasped and exploded; roof and masonry detonated in a thunder of dust. Oily columns cracked and buckled; black viscous floods spewed from severed pillars and cascaded down like tar-slick waterfalls, dousing bones and timbers. The floor heaved beneath them and the vault collapsed inwards in a cataclysmic implosion, a roaring maw of ruin bearing down on Bihan and Shadi.

Instinct seized him before reason could gather. He hauled Shadi's arm in a crushing grip, Rabia's ropes still slung across his shoulders with the stele harnessed against his back, and ran for the bas-reliefs. Bihan twisted to shield his good eye as chunks of ceiling pummelled the ground around them. Each step trembled the flagstones; dust older than empires choked their mouths. He felt the slab's cold teeth against his spine with every lurch. He wouldn't let it slip free. Couldn't.

They didn't look back. The apparitions were caught in the ruin; their spectral shrieks were swallowed by the avalanche of stone and oil. Montero's half-formed incantations were cut off by the roar, his pleas buried beneath falling masonry. Ahead, the carved wall promised the four secret doors and, with them, escape. For a breath, however, they were unreachable; invisible as if the world itself conspired to test them.

"Close your eyes, Shadi!" Bihan rasped. "Now!"

Silence fell like a curtain. The senses dimmed; the world became a husk in an aether-torn moment that Montero might've named as such. Then, as abruptly as it began, the four esoteric doors flickered into being behind them. They stumbled through and across the shattered remnants of Rabia's tomahawks—bent metal, splintered wood, relics of a valiant last stand. They climbed the rope, hearts hammering in their throats, and tumbled back into the vault that'd once held them captive. Silence reclaimed the necropolis. Only the echo of ragged breath and the distant, dying thunder of collapse remained.

Rabia's sacrifice lay beneath that ruin.

Bihan's palms burnt as they slid along the rope; friction bit into raw skin and the pain anchored him to the present. Shadi hauled himself up, knees scraped and sobbing, and leant against Bihan with the kind of collapse that carries both relief and ruin. Bihan set the basalt slab down; its impact sounded like a small, terrible victory, swallowed immediately by the vault's heavy quiet.

Collapsing by the jagged crevice, Bihan shut his only-working eye until galaxies burst behind his lid. Where his fingertips had once tingled, now both hands shook with a deep, unsettling vibration that rippled up his arms and consumed his body. He recalled Rabia's final words—saving his life again—and wondered what she truly meant. However, Bihan knew he'd never know unless he tracked down Darragh and entered another globe. Even then, the thaumaturge had warned that some feelings and secrets refused to bend to magic, and Bihan would never desecrate her memory with necromancy.

He thought of Fregor's grave and the vow he'd sworn never to let that hollowness return. Losing Rabia, however, was a different wound—shattering the very fabric of his being. He couldn't breathe; each gasp caught in a ravaged throat. He couldn't think; his mind whirled with agony. He couldn't remember his own name he'd borne.

A clammy hand brushed his shoulder. Shadi's touch was small and human, and it cracked him open; Bihan sobbed, a sound torn from the rawest part of him, until tears ran dry and the world sharpened again.

"The wyverns will be protected, on my honour." He rose, lifted the stele once more—its burden now heavier than stone and grief combined—and hurled it into the shimmering mercury that pooled in the vault. The metal swallowed the basalt with a hiss and splintering, the inscription vanishing into molten silence. "For Rabia," he breathed.

Two tasks remained, stark in his grief: send the wyverns to the safety of their kin, and hunt down the woman who dealt in beauty and betrayal until her name bled into silence.

XVII

A Secret Kept in Stone

The steady drip of wyrm oil onto Syrek's shattered remnants set the vault's slow metronome, a sickly rhythm that underscored Bihan and Shadi's isolation from Seaborne and from the cruel traps that had tried to bury them. If any pockets of aether had dulled their nerves during the escape, those numbings had long since bled away over the taut hours of waiting while Bihan shaped his plan in silence. Shadi, perched on his narrow haunches like a bird tense for flight, snapped his fingers; the soft click cleaved through the hush.

An idea, sharp and bright, struck him. The very spark that might free them. "I'd need your permission, of course," he prefaced, voice thin with nerves, "since you're the eye's master. It's necessary."

Bihan's knuckle went to the marble of his false eye as a reflex. With its original master gone, the orb no longer thrummed with latent power or flared with that disquieting light; it sat cool and inert, a hard thing of false sight and persistent irritation. *Rabia.* He pressed harder against the orb as if the name were an oath. Shadi set his twisted pearwood wand down before Bihan and, beside it, Montero's quarterstaff lay intact in a way that made Bihan's skin crawl.

"With these," Shadi said, gaining steadiness, "I can channel the magic for the spell. It'll take us out of here, anywhere you wish."

"And the vault?" Bihan asked, sweeping his gaze over the ruin's hollowed ribs.

"It'll remain," Shadi answered, eyes roaming their airless tomb. "Unless I decide otherwise. But don't you want any of these treasures? Not a single gold coin?"

The question hung and sank into the gloom. No breeze moved; no shaft of light found them. Their single lamp was Shadi's flickering fireball, a small, fiery sun in the palm of his hand. Bihan didn't need its light to recall the stele's ruin or the path it'd traced to the rare beasts they hunted. He saw the wyverns as clearly as if they crouched before him.

"No," he said, steady and flat. "I want my friend back. But since necromancy is something I can't bear; I will honour Rabia in the only way I know. That matters more than coin. Now—teleport us to the wyverns. After that, I'll be free to kill Captain Contreras."

"Very well." Shadi set the two sources of magic between them. "Hold them." Bihan closed his fingers around the cold wood. Shadi shut his eyes and drew breath. "*Harakuna beydaan... wyvern cave.*"

Something occult crawled beneath Bihan's skin, as if invisible script were being scored into his sinew. The sensation moved like a thousand ants up his right arm, then the left. Shadi's lids remained sealed; Bihan couldn't close his. He needed to watch. He listened for things that were not sounds—an echo left by a spell—while the drip of wyrm oil kept its slow, indifferent beat. Then the vault's atmosphere changed. He inhaled the scent of burning timber in rain, threaded with cinnamon, a smell he'd lived with alongside Shadi and his kind.

The unmistakable signature of magic.

A current shot from his fingertips to his heart, stamping a faster cadence into his blood before detonating outwards through every limb and pore. The jolt was harsher than any tremor the false eye had ever sent. Pain licked along the left side of his face as the fuchsia branching of Montero's orb snaked further down his cheek and jaw, a living scar.

The spell finished and the world closed.

Blackness swallowed them and they entered that vast void the ancients warned of; the Eternal Abyss where wraiths wandered and evildoers languished for eternity. The spell served no grander purpose than a simple teleport on a grander scale, if necessary, yet Bihan relished the thought of the crone's incredulous horror when she learnt how her son had squandered her life's work. Both the eye and the parchment were spent.

***

A warm breeze—the first breath of wind since the vault—kissed the nape of his neck in that void. Then the world snapped into focus: rough, damp cavern walls rose around them, the earthy tang of stone filling his nostrils. Relief, potent and disorienting, washed over him as recognition struck.

They'd arrived.

Shadi's eyes widened in horror. Bihan followed his gaze downwards, to where vivid purple vines pulsed across his skin, creeping from his false eye across his cheek and towards his collarbone. A brutal tattoo, alive and spreading, carved into his flesh. Fuel for the whispers and dark legends already circling his name. Yet beyond the sting he felt a grim certainty: Shadi had delivered them exactly where he'd longed to be.

The cave air carried a faint, briny hint of sea salt. Bihan edged closer to the jagged opening and looked out. Far below, the *Delphine* sat anchored in the bay's embrace, beautiful despite all circumstance. His gut twisted bitterly at the sight of a lone rowboat moored to a rickety pier, and he wondered if Sir Mathaeus had made it out safely.

"Bihan," Shadi whispered, trembling. "Don't make any sudden moves."

A heat like a furnace pressed against his back, smothering, unnatural. He remained facing the cave mouth, where the night's profound silence offered a crisp coolness in violent contest with that oppressive warmth. Had there been another exit, he might've clung to hope—but at this height, no natural wind could scorch like that.

This was no gust of nature. He knew what it was. He knew who exhaled that malevolent breath, but he dared not turn. The unseen presence rasped: a wet, labouring cough that sent a shiver down his spine.

"Thebian." The single word, deep and resonant, slid out of the darkness beside him.

Bihan's breath hitched as Sir Mathaeus stepped into view, his silhouette sharpening in the gloom. Instinct drove his hand to his weapons—seeking the reassuring weight of steel—but he found only empty air. The realisation struck Bihan like a physical blow; the reason why the paladin would be here. He was a hunter of magical creatures, human or otherwise.

"How did you find us?" he rasped, bracing for a fight he couldn't win.

"A powerful spell was cast," Mathaeus explained, in a calm and detached manner, as he drew his sword in a whisper of steel. "Its light pierced the sky and its scent—cinnamon—carried across Seaborne." He bowed his head to the blade, and at once a steady light bloomed along its length, scattering shadow. "My brothers and I are trained to—"

"*Shh!*" Shadi hissed, pressing a scarred finger to his lips, eyes darting to the deeper dark. "It'll wake!"

Bihan turned slowly, sweat beading on his brow, his legs trembling with anxiety and hurt. His one good eye adjusted to the gloom just as the blade's glow revealed the cavern's formidable prize.

Mathaeus' gasp echoed, reverent and horrified all at once. "By the divine... it cannot be a dragon."

The creature stirred above its lone, luminescent egg—an orb stark white, glowing faintly from within. Its wings, leathery and bat-like, joined its forelimbs, and its long body curled sinuous as a serpent. Regal purple scales shimmered beneath the golden light; its talons gleamed like burnished gold.

"A wyvern," Bihan whispered, his tone edged with reverence. "Only one."

"If you know its kind, then you must know how to kill it," Mathaeus replied, brandishing his sword with quiet purpose. "That's all we need."

"To slay dragon-kin would be a shame," Bihan growled, clamping a hand on the paladin's hilt. "It wasn't born of magic. No more mystical than a lizard."

"*Shh!*" Shadi warned, desperation souring the hiss.

Mathaeus faltered, lowering his blade a fraction. "I thought wyverns were children's fables. Legends to give peasants hope of glimpsing something akin to a dragon in their lifetime. Before the sapphire dragon of the south devastated my city, at least. Rumour claims a dragon and a desert wyrm once mated, producing only two wyverns: brother and sister. Slender odds lured a handful of stubborn pathfinders to chase phantoms into the wilds, while the rest, shackled by indolence, dismissed the chase as a fool's errand, unwilling to risk home for myth."

"Mundane hatchlings, as I said," Bihan muttered.

"Dragons were Mystics once," Mathaeus countered. "Magic runs through their veins, and through these creatures born of lust. Those bones must be the brother's. This sleeper, the sister. That egg, their inbred spawn."

"All that by looking?" Bihan frowned.

"By study," Mathaeus said sharply. "Libraries teach truths—"

A faint stir froze him.

The wyvern shifted like some old hound, roused from a nightmare, its hot breath thickening the air. The three men stiffened, lungs shallow, their hearts thundering. Bihan's mind screamed for Rabia's wit—the voice that'd commanded manticores, the cunning he sorely lacked.

The creature growled, low and resonant, a sound that rolled through stone. Mathaeus stepped forwards instinctively, raising his divine blade, shielding Bihan from the creature. Then her eyes opened. Ancient and luminous, the pupils narrowing into predatory slits. She weighed them each in turn, lifting her serpentine neck with regal judgement.

Bihan felt the truth settle coldly against his skin: he would fit neatly inside her cavernous maw.

"Stand down, Sir Mathaeus," Shadi whispered, urgency trembling in his tone. "We don't want to harm her."

"Quiet, Mystic. I owe you nothing." Mathaeus' reply sliced the air like tempered steel.

"You owe *me* nothing," Bihan hissed. "Your debt was paid. Begone, D'Laurentice. Go home to your golden city."

"No." In a blur, the knight surged forwards, slipping from Bihan's desperate grasp.

The wyvern reacted instantly. She spread her leathery wings and retched a torrent of dark, viscous blood across their faces—an unmistakable confession of illness. With a resonant clang, Mathaeus struck her hind leg with the flat of his blade. She convulsed violently, tail coiling around her luminous egg, gouging furrows into the cave floor as she spun.

Despite her size, Mathaeus moved with deadly grace. But her lithe body anticipated him. A hind leg lashed out, flinging him into the mound of her mate's bleached bones. She roared—a grieving, primal bellow—then clawed and snapped, never loosening her coil around the egg. Recovering, the paladin raised his holy blade and sliced into her flank. A searing light erupted, cauterising the wound before it bled.

"Stand down, knight!" Bihan bellowed, tasting hot, metallic blood on his lips. "Shadi, do something!"

"I can't!" Shadi cried, despair cracking his tone. "Not without risking her life!"

Bihan Alihanson surveyed the desperate tableau—the frenzied paladin, the ailing wyvern, the egg hidden in her draconian tail. Unarmed, he felt hollow. Powerless. So, he abandoned strength and sought weakness: the alabaster egg, its shell marred by a jagged black bolt.

For Rabia, he urged himself.

In a silent crouch, he darted forwards, footsteps swallowed by the damp cave floor.

The wyvern's jaws snapped shut around Mathaeus with a thunderous crack. He hammered her snout with his pommel, but her grip only tightened, dark blood oozing from between sharp teeth. As she reared back, her tail shifted—just enough.

Bihan scaled her flank, sandals sliding on ridged scales. He reached the egg, tore it free, and tumbled backwards, clutching it to his chest. Shadi's intuitive ward softened the fall, and together they scrambled towards the cavern mouth.

The wyvern unleashed a shriek that split stone, then flung the stunned knight aside. He crashed back into the bones as she advanced, ragged breath shaking her frame, eyes burning with fury, talons raking for her stolen brood.

"Great mother of dragon-kin," Bihan panted, chest heaving, "I never wanted this."

Her eyes narrowed, commanding, regal. "You stole my child. Return him or suffer."

Bihan swallowed hard. "Grant us a moment, and he'll be unharmed." He held the egg at arm's length. "Step closer, and your bloodline ends here."

A hiss rumbled in her chest. "You *dare* threaten me?"

"We came in peace," Shadi interjected, stepping forwards. "We found Freja Torbjörn's stele. Her kin died so we could reach you—to protect your hatchling."

The wyvern recoiled, tail twitching, and hurled a puddle of blackish ichor at their feet. Her stance wavered, serpentine eyes rolling in a harrowing display of agony. Dark blood pooled at her claws—clots of viscera and ragged flesh, the same plague that'd ruined Aledhyn and now the Imperium's capital.

Bihan edged back from the stench, the egg tight to his chest. Mathaeus stiffened, the light fading from his blade as revulsion seized his features. He sheathed the weapon and drifted into the shadows of her great flank, silent as a wraith.

Bihan's breath hitched, recalling the exchange in Darragh's shop, but before he could speak, Shadi answered for him. "If exposed, their lungs would shrivel, their scales would crumble at fever's touch—to plague. She's dying, Bihan."

The wyvern dipped her neck in a bone-rattling sigh, stirring dust motes from the cavern floor. Bihan pressed the egg against his chest, memory flashing of Montero's vomit in Syrek. "It was because of his arrival, wasn't it? You must've felt him—a powerful Mystic."

A dry chuckle cracked from her throat, ending in a hacking cough that sprayed black blood. "I felt nothing. This sickness killed my mate. Now it devours me." Bihan's heart throbbed with grief for Rabia and her quest. "But not my son," she hissed, nodding towards the alabaster egg. "Let me bleed willingly for him. Coat his shell in this plague. Slay me before he hatches. It's the only way."

A slender radiance swelled from the cavern depths, bathing her in otherworldly light. She glared as it grew.

"I won't," Bihan said steadily.

She rose to her full, regal height despite each ragged breath. "You must," she roared, eyes sweeping over Bihan, Shadi, and the shadow behind her. "I see turmoil and honour in you all. You're bound to oaths sworn, to those you cherish, to vengeance yet unclaimed. But true honour is more than mercy. It is the courage to strike when the moment demands. This is that moment. Only by taking that step will your vows be vindicated, your duties fulfilled; a friend's death not in vain."

Shadi slid his pearwood wand into his sleeve and planted his quarterstaff, choosing mercy over steel. Impatience rippled through the wyvern's scaly flesh, talons lifting in silent promise of death.

"Wait!" Bihan seized the breath between. "My companion's magic can heal you."

"No," she rasped, crushing hope. "No magic can staunch this plague. I'd have taken my life long ago if not for him. I feared leaving my son to this merciless world. I'd have let my blood soak his egg sooner, but I dreaded the risk of suicide sullying the sacred vow sworn on my diseased life force. In this sickly blood, no spark of divinity remains to transform him, to steel him against this curse."

Legends say vows forged in such fierce anguish draw divine favour, a spark of old-world magic woven through a warrior's pledge. Bihan's oath on the crucifix crackled with that ancient force, and upon her death, so too would the wyvern's.

"I've scoured every alternative," the great beast continued, "only this one remains."

With a wet, sickening thud, her massive head snapped from her neck and crashed at Bihan's sandalled feet, splashing dark ichor across the stone. The blade's holy fire had sealed the ragged edges of the wound but hadn't closed it fully.

Biting back fury, Bihan thought grimly: had the blade's fire wholly sealed her wound, her sacrifice would've been in vain. Yet he forced the rage down, released the egg, and planted both feet beside it. He turned away from Mathaeus, drenched in blood so thick that it gleamed like wyrm oil.

The alabaster shell soaked up its mother's life. Crimson rivulets spread across the surface.

"The debt is paid," Mathaeus intoned, his voice drained of feeling as he sheathed the glowing blade. He nodded towards the blood-soaked egg. "Destroy it before it hatches."

"Destroy it?" Bihan's laugh was edged with disbelief. "This child lives. I name him Rabio, in honour of his kind's sworn protector and my dearest friend. He'll survive, free of the plague that claimed his kin. The last of his kind, like me."

On the utterance of his name, the shell cracked. Beginning at the black bolt, lines spread like veins, blooming outwards. A tiny wyvern, vibrant green and no larger than a lapdog, tumbled free. He blinked ancient eyes and yawned into the cavern's glow. His colour echoed the dragon fabled to sire his line—a living testament to hope.

Bihan met Rabio's gaze and felt warmth stir in his chest, unfamiliar yet undeniable. Purpose. He'd honoured an oath and Rabia's memory and vowed to guard this hatchling with his life. Not sequestered in distant lands beyond reach of man or Laic, but at his side until death, and onwards into the rise of a new generation in the Realm.

Beyond protection, however, one desire and vow burnt clearer than ever: vengeance.

XVIII

Where Oaths are Honoured

At the narrow, rickety pier the quartet boarded Sir Mathaeus' battered rowboat with reverent caution. The hull, pocked and scarred, sloshed seawater across tired planks; a single misstep would have sent them tumbling. Bihan climbed in first, feet slipping into a cold, briny pool as he cradled the hatchling to his chest. Shadi and Mathaeus followed, seizing the worn oars, the wood slick with salt. The notorious barbarian cooed a soft, rumbling lullaby—his deep timbre nearly lost beneath the timbers' complaining groan.

Mathaeus' nostrils flared at cinnamon's sickly sweetness. His jaw tightened; his gaze flicked between Rabio and Shadimtha, every rigid gesture betraying a battle inside him. Contempt warred with duty. Bihan tightened his grip on Rabio, forcing himself to breathe slow and steady.

They pushed off. Each heave of the oars drew the *Delphine* nearer: a shadowed leviathan anchored in the bay, its barnacled prow a siege wall against the morning. Mathaeus braced a gauntleted hand on the tarred ladder that swung from the carrack's side, impatience coiling beneath his hollow composure. Rabio stirred. Tiny claws skittered along Bihan's forearm as the hatchling wriggled free and clambered onto his shoulder, emerald scales whispering against his stubble.

The wyvern nuzzled into the crook of his neck, a reptilian grin twisting his snout as if he recognised him already. Bihan pressed his cheek to his flank, an unspoken vow in the gesture. His scales were cool and hard like river-burnished stones yet throbbed with a living heat beneath, as if molten blood ran close to the surface.

Across the cove, Seaborne's ramparts shimmered through mist. Lanterns winked like stubborn stars; laughter and hurried feet drifted faintly ashore. A tightening in Bihan's chest blurred his sight. He swallowed, tasting brine and an ache that wouldn't be named: Rabia's face, and the hollow where her voice had been. They were leaving her to memory and the ruined city that'd buried her.

Rabio watched Seaborne's glittering expanse and then the great carrack with boundless wonder. Each scaled muscle in his small, lithe body pulsed with excitement, as if every plank and sail made perfect sense to him. His wide, ancient eyes held a depth no elder could match; that wisdom made the hatchling's childish awe all the more luminous. Bihan felt the current of Rabio's reverence as plainly as he felt the animal's weight against his shoulder. No words passed between them. Only the electric insistence of a newly formed bond.

A subtle warmth seeped through Bihan's ribs where Rabio pressed close. The hatchling's secretions left a cool, slick trail on his skin that tingled in equal parts discomfort and comfort. Two last-of-their-kind souls mirrored one another: grief and hope braided together before a single breath was even taken. They became a single, fierce heartbeat of purpose. That purpose blazed in both their eyes: vengeance. A raw hunger to rend Camila Callo Contreras from life and consign her beauty and betrayal to the sea.

"Bihan," Shadi whispered, tugging at the fringe of his sporran, the tremor in his tone thin with pleading. "You don't have to do this. We've honoured Rabia. Let it end here."

Bihan's lips thinned into a grim smile. "No. I'll see that bitch's beauty crushed beneath the Shamrock's keel." The words left him like a promise. "Camila Callo dies today."

Dawn's molten-gold fingers crept over the eastern peaks, bathing the *Delphine* in an ethereal wash. The air warmed enough to dry their sodden footwear. With catlike grace, Bihan and Rabio climbed the tarred ladder and slipped aboard the sleeping carrack without sound. Pyrates sprawled across deck and tumbled in shadowed holds, a pair of dainty, sandalled feet dangled from the crow's nest, and the collective breath of lazy seamen rumbled like grinding stones. Bihan knew these weathered sailors from Aledhyn. Camila had left no shortage of allies. He looked to Shadi and Mathaeus; silent confirmation passed between them.

Camila's army was ready, but so was their vengeance.

The sun hovered as a perfect semicircle above the horizon; its fiery reflection skittering across the bay's wavelets, scattering liquid gold over each crest. Wispy clouds drifted aside to reveal a sky that shifted from pearl grey into an impossible bluish-green—greener, as old mariners swore, over the Shamrock Sea.

Bihan raised a hand in a casual wave. Rabio mirrored the gesture, precise and immediate—a private echo of their covenant. Their footsteps whispered across deck planks. Even Mathaeus' armoured gait fell muted, a courtesy for slipping among sleeping foes. At the hatchway, the chorus of snores thinned; ragged breaths faltering as dawn chased away night.

"Heard the Vizier's dead," a pyrate mumbled from below, slack with sleep. "Unloyal as a cat, that one."

"Disloyal," another yawned, the cavernous sound shaking loose dust in the darkness.

"Who?" came a third voice, half-awake.

"Never mind," the yawner said. "Is Captain Contreras keeping the blockade? I'm bored as sin."

"You took first watch. Your fault," the first scoffed. "We'll starve on that cloying Chardonnay before she stands us down. Tastes like dirty feet and rust. Nah, we're stuck here a while longer. Take the easy way out, I say."

A twitch ran along Bihan's jaw at the pyrate's casual dismissal of his hard-won prize. He longed for the sharp crack of Camila's tongue to scold them. Only then would he slit her throat... and theirs.

Sir Mathaeus slid his sword free; its light dimmed into a matte grey promise of death. He crouched low, and, with the predatory silence of a huntsman, began a deadly ballet—throats taken one by one. Bodies slumped without cry, hammocks and ragged blankets cradling men into final sleep. Shadi planted his quarterstaff at the hatch and kept his wand haloed like a watchful sentinel. Bihan stood between them, eye flicking from hatch to knight to the yawning dialogue below; the hatch was a doorway to chaos, ready to erupt with every stolen breath.

"Never understood that," the third pyrate muttered, sleep still coating his words. "How's dying easy? You suffer, you gasp... then nothingness forever. Seems rather dull."

"You wouldn't feel, hear or see a thing, mung-bean," his companion, the yawner, cut in flatly. "It couldn't be dull."

"But that's what makes it dull," the third sighed, a philosophical weight dragging through dawn's chill.

Sir Mathaeus rejoined them, his boots leaving faint dark stains as he moved with lethal precision. He bent to the hatch, gauntlet hovering over the lock. Bihan gave a curt nod. Camila would be waiting in the garish quarters once occupied by the false captain with the jolly belly. They'd overwhelm the watchmen in an instant, bolstered by magic and divine might. Above them all, Rabio perched on the Last Barbarian's shoulder, a living omen certain to unnerve every eye it met. Bihan imagined how Rabia might've spun the image into legend, whispered in taverns for generations.

His jaw tightened as he readied his fists: the right hand closing into an iron knot, the ruined left clinging to its clawed half-form. Rabia's name echoed in his mind with every tightening of his jaw, the gold replacement tooth scraping against enamel. *I am vengeance*, he vowed. Mathaeus' gloved fingers brushed the brass handle, then Bihan struck first, shoving the knight aside and driving his sandalled foot into the door. It burst into splinters, jagged shards raining down in a thunderous crash. Down the narrow stairs the startled watchmen tumbled, fumbling for their cutlasses. Rabio hissed, talons flaring, needle-fine teeth bared. Dust and fear thickened the air; each heartbeat thudded like a war drum.

A cruel laugh then rang from above—the dainty, sandalled feet swaying in the crow's nest. "One by one you slit their throats," Captain Contreras called, her words slicing through the din. "And piece by piece, your soul dwindled to a sliver." She stood arms akimbo, haloed by dawn's molten light; contempt etched into every line of her posture. "You should've died on that crucifix and let the crows feast," she sneered, eyes gleaming with wicked satisfaction.

Bihan's gaze fixed on her flawless features, the deceptive softness masking the demon beneath. Mathaeus raised his sword, steady and ready, but Bihan stepped in front of him, shifting his weight in silent defiance. Camila smirked and inspected her manicured nails as if they were sharp weapons.

"Your words were honeyed, Camila, but your intent curdled the instant they passed your lips. Toppling Toussaint? A pedestrian ambition in wake of his support. Aspiring to rival mine own exploits? Laughable. You needed a far more compelling pitch."

"*My* own," she corrected. "Leave your archaicism buried with the Amity Era."

A growl vibrated Bihan's chest. "Regardless," he said, teeth bared, "for all your pride, you failed to claim this creature. Yet I did—flawlessly."

Rabia's silver tongue flitted at the edges of memory, but now he leant on a different strength: his own charisma. His legend had always rested as much on charm as on muscle and steel. Deprived of weapons, he adapted. Confidence bloomed unexpectedly in his chest. Archaic speech or not, he felt good.

Deliberately, he turned his shoulder, letting dawn's light gleam across Rabio's emerald scales. For the briefest moment, Camila's mask cracked. Wide-eyed yearning washed over her like a child glimpsing something forbidden in a brothel's chaos. With inhuman grace, she rappelled down the rope, chin trembling as she reached out—then recoiled, covering her mouth. Her gaze clung to the hatchling, oblivious to Shadi's humming wand and quarterstaff, oblivious even to Mathaeus' poised blade.

"Magnificent," she whispered, pupils blown wide. "With that creature, I'll be unstoppable. I'll restore the Imperium to the glory of the pure-blooded Scions of Wolvesmìre. Imperatrix Camila Callo Contreras the First."

"His name is Rabio," Bihan said, scars tightening as his nose wrinkled. "His namesake lies dead in Syrek's ruins because of your ambitions."

She ignored him, stepping closer, fingers poised to claim Rabio. Bihan caught her wrist in an iron grip.

"Touch him," he growled, "and I'll break every bone in this pretty hand."

Her smirk slithered back. She swept her gaze over him then nodded towards another hatch. With a sudden crack it burst open behind Bihan, and a tide of scurvy-riddled pyrates flooded into the light, scimitars clenched between yellowed teeth, knives glinting like hungry vipers.

"Fool," Captain Contreras chuckled, low and humourless. "I'm always ten steps ahead. Who do you think tipped Montero off about Rabia the Rogue-turned-Banker? Who told him you'd seek her out after Fregor the Cutpurse's death?"

Bihan's lips peeled back in a snarl. "I know. You've already said as much."

Camila drew herself to full height, spine like a drawn bow, eyes glinting with cruel fire. "Then I'll say it again. Every twist of this tale is by my hand—even Montero's demise. You think me callow, but you've yet to grasp my reach. I know your weaknesses and your strengths. Vengeance and grief drive you, but honour propels you forwards."

A tremor rippled down Bihan's spine. Rabio hissed from his shoulder, claws raking faint lines into his skin.

"I know you better than you know yourself," Camila went on, eyes flicking with contempt over Mathaeus and Shadi. "Better than he knows his prayers, better than Shadimtha knows his mother's crushing ambition. Your legend is every-thing to me, Bihan Alihanson. I'll love you for an eternity because of it. But if you refuse to surrender that wyvern—here and now—then I'll unite us in another way. By feasting on your gorgeous flesh."

Bihan met her promise with a straight, dead stare. Her words stirred nothing in him—no fear, no anger, no surprise. Whatever sparks of empathy remained lay reserved for his companions, and even those were scarce. Once he'd commanded the finest journeymen and women; now he led a rag-tag band: a wyvern, a magus, and a man of the cloth with a sword. Yet facing Camila's scurvy-ridden pyrates, Bihan felt only a fierce surge of pride and unshakeable resolve. He tipped his head towards the crow's nest, and Rabio launched into the dawn air with a joyous warble instead of a roar.

"Let the feast begin, then," Bihan declared.

He charged, headbutting the nearest pyrate and sending him sprawling, then followed with a bloodied fist that caved a man's sternum in a sickening crack. Shadi loosed a flare of arcane energy towards Camila as she scrambled for the rope to intercept Rabio. The cord went up in an instant, fire devouring the hemp, and she shrieked as she fell, sandals bursting apart on the deck.

Sir Mathaeus drove another pyrate's back into the mast, splintering wood with the force. His matte-grey blade swept through fingers and jugular in one brutal arc, then lodged in the timber. The dying man clutched his throat as blood gushed; Mathaeus, with horrifying precision, plunged his hand into the wound and tore the tongue free. He ripped his sword loose with a wet rasp, ducked a wild cut, and pivoted on one knee to bisect an elfiran pyrate in a single devastating stroke.

Across the deck, Camila sprinted barefoot, crimson footprints marking her frantic flight. She lunged for a rope ladder and climbed with desperate haste, every muscle straining. The warriors of the *Delphine* were blind to her escape, enthralled by Mathaeus' butchery, but Bihan saw—and barrelled through falling bodies, Shadi carving a path beside him with arcs of crackling magic.

He flung himself up the rope ladder, muscles screaming, until his ruined hand slipped on the tarred hemp. His foot missed the rung. Panic clutched him as the world dropped away. Cold sweat stung his brow; the deck rose fast, a splintered grave of blood and wood.

He braced for impact. Then—a joyous squawk rang clear above the din. A rope zipped past and snapped taut. Bihan seized it with desperate strength. Overhead, Rabio spiralled, talons ready, and dove into a scurvy-ridden pyrate, wrenching a dagger free with his teeth before returning to the crow's nest, guardian and victor.

Bihan shook off the near-fall and surged upwards again, fury hauling him towards Camila's silhouette. She jeered, blowing a raspberry of triumph as Rabio stood serenely at her feet. That calm struck Bihan harder than her mockery. The hatchling's composure was a silent rebuke to her frenzy, and it steeled his resolve.

When Bihan hauled himself over the edge, Camila and Rabio were locked in an uncanny communion. Their gazes tangled in silence: hers a fevered craving, like the relief of bathwater after days in the mines, while the newborn wyvern studied her with calculating intrigue. It wasn't hatred in Rabio's eyes, but a chilling curiosity born of principle. She'd orphaned him. Justice demanded her death.

Bihan felt that unspoken logic even if he couldn't articulate it; to feel doesn't always grant the power to speak. He sensed their shared turmoil like an echo in his own chest: grief, vengeance, honour, all braided into a single bond. Vengeance and honour propelled Bihan Alihanson with crystalline purpose. He needed only the final push.

Then something in Camila snapped. Her eyes widened with primal hunger. She spat at his sandalled feet and lunged for Rabio with an animal cry. Bihan moved faster. He caught her wrists and crushed them. Bones splintered, flesh tore, and he wrenched until her palms came apart from her wrists in one violent motion. He'd warned her.

Her shriek ripped through the dawn as her mangled hands dangled grotesquely before her quivering arms. Blood spurted from her nose and lips; veins writhed across her forehead like bursting rivers. In a last frenzy she hurled herself at him, but he shouldered her aside. She struck the balustrade with a dull crack. Rabio dropped the stolen dagger into Bihan's good hand, then settled above them in silent vigilance.

Bihan knelt—not in reverence, but finality. This was the woman he'd pursued across the world. And for an instant, as his fingers touched her skin, he almost forgot what she was.

Almost.

The dagger swept across her throat in one clean motion. No triumph. Just steel through flesh, severing windpipe and artery. A gruesome gurgle rattled as her body spasmed. He spared her tongue, unwilling to desecrate her further as Mathaeus had done, and watched the life drain from her beautiful hazel eyes. The whites flushed red; tears pooling and mingling with crimson as she choked on her own blood. A silent, pleading question bloomed in her frightened stare, a desperate final prayer for mercy he wouldn't grant. With a wet death rattle, she stilled.

Calm washed over him—completion. The fulfillment of his honour-bound vow. Captain Contreras was dead.

Even as the blue deformity in her iris clouded into the hoary white of death, Bihan admitted she remained beautiful. A person deserving of his mocking title of "Beauty."

A magnificent façade over a ruined, monstrous soul.

The smoke of battle had only just thinned when Shadi slumped against a cluster of intact barrels, exhaustion claiming him at last. His scarred forearm, newly etched with runes, pulsed faintly beneath his skin as he sank into a deep, healing sleep. At the helm, Sir Mathaeus sat unarmoured, his discarded plate a mute witness to the violence past, while his black tunic billowed in the cove's gentle breeze. Rabio, the last wyvern, returned to perch on Bihan's shoulder, nuzzling against the colourful and magical tattoos that spiralled down his jaw and throat. Victory, then, seemed both fragile and complete.

Bihan moved with the wyvern to stand beside the knight. Mathaeus' wounds had closed, yet his eyes bore a distant, haunted sheen. He absently fingered the empty phial once sewn into his forearm—a relic of torture endured, never forgotten. Bihan recognised another crucifix of pain in the man's past but chose silence over questions. Together they faced south, shoulders squared, companions bound by scars.

A soft breeze lifted Bihan's hair, brushing his skin like a promise of change. He thought of the future—where it might lead, and with whom. Rabia was avenged, his crucifixion repaid in blood, his oaths honoured, the dragon-kin line preserved.

With debts fulfilled, no path demanded him now, save the one he chose.

He wouldn't abandon Rabio to the desolation of the northern wastes, nor bear the scented weight of orange-blossom memories in Aledhyn's familiar streets. His gaze lingered on the horizon, where the Shamrock Sea kissed the southern continent's jagged silhouette. He remembered the plague that razed Aledhyn, claimed Rabio's parents, and then crept south towards the dragon-guarded capital. An army of loyalists and a self-styled imperator loomed there—destined for ruin or redemption. Yet in the calm after carnage, Bihan felt a stirring of hope. They would face it together: magus, knight, barbarian, and wyvern, bound by trial into one.

Rabio squawked softly, emerald eyes gleaming with agreement, and flapped his leathery wings. Bihan offered a slow nod, meeting Mathaeus' pale, steady gaze before glancing at

Shadi's sleeping form. Dawn's full light spilt across the deck, gilding splintered timbers and glistening scales alike.

And so, with hearts tempered by fire and steel, they set sail with hope their only true north.